Coyote Rebooted

Coyote is up & running as his grassland paradise
is run over by the monster industrial machine,
but he has 30,000 years of trick experience
with monkey wrenches and false faces.

Yulalona Lopez

Books by Yulalona Lopez
  Night Wolves
  Tropomorphoses
  Coyote Redivivus
  Coyote Redux
  Coyote Remasked
  Ambimorphoses (2009)

Books from Calliope Press in 2007-08
  Waste Heat, by Violet Reason
  Musings, ed. by Crawford Washington
  Masks, ed. by Crawford Washington
  Waiting for Better Times (in Bulgaria), by Conor Ciaran
  Fragments, by A. M. Caratheodory
  Light from a Vanished Forest, by A. M. Caratheodory
  Amphibian Dreams, by A. M. Caratheodory
  Tears from the Sun: Lucifer Burning, by Marcus Ryan
  Two Diaries, by Marcus Ryan

From the Classic Library
  Masque of the Red Rash, by Emerson Alan Poe
  The Man in the Ironic Mask, by Alexandre Dumblas
  The Mask of Fu La Mancha, by Vladislaw Roamer
  Itsayaya Jones and the Crystal Mask of the Pintopup People
  Battlecrafter Mask, by Don Ponderous
  Concrete Jungle Masks of New York, by Rudee Giuliani
  Chia Mask Garden Pet, by Victory Swenson
  The Mask of Power, by Calvin Hobbes
  Behind the Mask of Civility, by Forbes X. Clarke
  Curse of the Ancient Monkey Mask, by Quichua Sinna

Coyote Rebooted

Coyote is up & running as his grassland paradise
is run over by the monster industrial machine,
but he has 30,000 years of trick experience
with monkey wrenches & false faces.

First Alternate Title:
Coyote Recidivist
Back to the Basics of Bulltricks

Second Alternate Title:
Coyote Reflux
Strange Myths and Weird Tales
of the Original Coyote As Regurgitated by Himself

The Translithic Trickster Turns!

(Cosmic Life Edition)

Yulalona Lopez

Illustrations by Oniotario Lopez

Mozart & Reason Wolf
Sarasota 2009

Acknowledgments

Several of these works have been published on internet sites
out of desperation. Forgive them.

Book Design by Ryan Garcia Calusa, Tallevast, Florida
Designers@RianGarciaCalusa.com
Original drawings copyright by Oniotario Lopez

Editing by Muses Books, Sarasota, Florida
Editor@3Musesbooks.com

Imprint: Mozart & Reason Wolfe, Ltd., Wilmington, Delaware
Mozart@ReasonWolf.com

Yulalona@Itsayaya.com

Publishers Cataloging-in-Publication data
Yulalona Lopez, 1969—

Coyote Remasked/Yulalona Lopez
I. Title. PS3553.A644A898 2009

ISBN 0-911385-44-4 (paper)

978-0-911385-44-1 (paper)

Manufactured in the United States of America

Dedications

To the Coyote Being behind every living being.

To Precious Woulfe, for being.

To Margaret Ryan, for being, oh, *Je ne sais quoi.*

To Dvorah Levy, for being patient for a Jewish Coyote (And why not? There are Jewish wolves in Israel).

And, finally, to our loyal, beloved readers (alphabetically): Samir Aliev, Anonymous, Petar Baldjiev, Mike Barnes, Tara Brice (who dried the pages in the sun first), Jim Chandler (who rebuilt a computer to read the pdf file), Craig & Linda Dillard (who looked at some of the pictures), Bret & Susan Dowell, Valya Dobrolubova, Sonja Duenwald, Shapari Enshayan, Sarah Featherkile, Ronnie & Olga Gabriel (who used their copy as fox bait), Christyann Helm, Amy Ihrke, Incognito, Twila Jacobsen (who read it at her new job), Erina, Minori, Neil, & Yoshie Keefe (who asked for more Uzume), Kathleen List (who ordered a copy for the library), James Luck (who hasn't actually bought a copy), Johanna Metzger (who actually returned her copy), Magneto, Linda-Grace Martin-Schaff, Lena Nieman (who drew on her copy), B. N. Patterson, Pseudonymous, Joyce Schulte (who cleaned the garage to get a free copy), Unknown, Karen Walter (who used her copy as a ping pong racket), Janet & Leonard Wampler (who sold their copy to the neighbor), Carl & Elaine Wittbecker, and Victoria Zavala B. (who promised to read it after I died and it became more valuable).

—YLL

Coyote Rebooted

Contents

Preface About Face

Professor Merton Mirthless, Grace Sheauga, and Simla Featherkile engage in a conversation about Coyote, in the conference room of Calliope Press just off the Tamiami Trail in Sarasota. It is 90 degrees outside and sunny. Featherkile is a tall blonde with a beautiful smile, the guest editor of the book, a ground-breaking feminist and noted author of the *Cup and the Frying Saucer* and *Women Who Mate with Wolves*. She sits across from Mirthless, a tall, slim, impeccably-dressed caricature of a professor with a strong profile and flowing dark hair, grey at the temples, without the hint of a smile. Professor Mirthless teaches Southern European Culture at Florida Modern University in Sandville. At the end of the table, Sheauga, a short dark woman with lively dark eyes, is scanning part of the manuscript. A member of the Iroquois Nation, she is a senior engineer with Sverdrop AG in Stockholm with a specialty of air-water systems in arcologies.

Featherkile: "What is Coyote for you, Prof. Mirthless?"

Mirthless: "Coyote is pantophagous— "

F: "What?"

M: "It means he eats anything—and he is rectopathic."

F: "He's a psychotic asshole?"

M: "Oh, good heavens, no, it means he is easily hurt emotionally."

F: "No, I mean essentially. Is he dog, god, myth, or fiction?"

M: "None, just a character who is always quick with a firk on a fleak."

F: "Huh?"

M: "He tricks women who are not too bright, like book commentators."

F: "Trick?" the smile dimmed.

M: "Yes, into believing that his stories are innocent and educational."

F: "Are you a solipsist or just a clueless asshole? Pushing your own version of his-story, no doubt."

M: "Just what I would expect a wind-breaking femalist to say."

Sheauga: "Pardon me, I would like to answer that question with another question. Why is Coyote working on computers in these stories?"

M: "Yes, why do we have to have Coyote driving cars? That's ridiculous!"

F: "Both interesting questions. If Coyote, and his human lessons, are to survive, he has to adapt to new times, new media and new markets. Besides, story-telling has always explored the ways and limits of technology through social change."

M: "Coyote is not relevant. These stories are not even amusing as fantasies."

S: "Why wouldn't he be relevant?"

F: "Remember, Coyote is an archetype. He is an expected character in traditional stories. And, characters from the past can help us understand the present."

M: "By ruining it?"

F: "By showing us how some actions can ruin it, yes. But, he makes the present clear, by his seeing a situation now for the first time, in ways that we who grew up in it might not see it. Think, the human story has changed little, in its essence, over time. Yes, I know, cars, computers, chainsaws, the tools change, but these are tools to help us live, work, eat, sleep …"

S: "Coyote engages, involves, the listeners, or readers, as the story interacts and reflects our lives. The story-teller does this."

F: "The world is confusing and ambiguous, and Coyote makes it more simple and sure."

M: "Why does Coyote have so much trouble with masks? He is always having to get and wear masks."

F: "Okay, he—"

S: "I wonder, too. How does his mate create masks as she, well, on the fly? Why can't Coyote or others do that?"

F: "Well, we should talk about masks—"

M: "Why is so much attention wasted on masks?"

F: "Masks have occupied the entire human history of art, possibly 60,000 years. The first art was animal sketches and masks."

M: "But, where are those masks?"

F: "They did not survive as well as rock or cave art."

M: "I thought only sedentary societies, farmers, had masks?"

F: "No, hunters and gatherers, fisherfolk, pastoralists, on almost all continents, all had masks."

M: "Why did they disappear? Why aren't they used now?"

F: "They didn't disappear. The Greeks and Romans used them in theatrical performances. The Chinese, Japanese, Europeans, for festivals."

S: "Masks have the power to alter your identity, so that they confer the power of the spirit on you. As an object, a mask is a means of expression and a form of secrecy."

M: "But why does one need an object? We know that children and politicians make and wear masks of their own flesh. That is just part of their identities."

F: "Masks, a physical mask, provides a focus, an external form of communication, apart from the self."

S: "Look at this image of a rock painting from China. This is an oval mask of some divinity, perhaps. It is an archetypal facemask. Here from the Lascaux grotto in France is a bison charging a birdman. And, look at this mask. It is a man with the head of an elk and a man with the head of a horse—this from 6,000 years ago. Look at the colors! Red is a dominant color, perhaps it means blood, or life. It is a zoomorphic mask that may refer to a totemic animal who was the origin of the people. This mask would have been worn during dances and ceremonies. It would evoke communication from the supernatural, through the mask. For the viewers it would bring a legend to life. It would reveal the face of the god founder."

F: "That's a nice book. I saw an image in it earlier. In the Cave of the Fox is a human figure with the face and mane of a bison; he is playing a stringed instrument. The mask conceals the identity of the wearer and reveals the god. The mask can explain to the viewers those events that may be inexplicable, such as snowstorms or volcanoes that kill people. A large part of the identity of any group is defined by myths, whether they are of the primacy of salmon or the neutrality of science.

M: "So, you think the invisible or the eternal reality of myth is closer to truth than the everyday life?"

S: "No, Together they add to truth, neither canceling or replacing the other."

M: "Why do only humans wear masks?"

S: "They do not. Humans do wear masks of animals, but animals wear masks of humans. This is a common language shared by both to explore the unknowns of the other; the speakers form a dialectic."

M: "Oh, floxigelder. Any other combinations in that book?"

S: "Yes, here is the body of a deer with the head of a bison. Here is the body of a human with the head of a bird and the feet of an animal. Here is a bear with the beak of a bird. Here is one from Seminole Canyon, Texas, a birdman with wings."

M: "So, it's men and animals?"

S: "No, women, too. A woman being impregnated by a deer masked man. In Algeria, men with the head of a mushroom, a flower, a fruit. Perhaps this reflected the use of hallucinogens by hunters. In Australia a potato-man. In Amazonia a yam-spirit. Some masks had elements of the sun, moon or stars."

F: "The Kwakwakawakw on the northwest coast had masks of

lightning or clouds as well as animals; these were part of their crest poles sometimes."

S: "Quite so. When an individual puts on a mask, she acquires the power of the spirit and can act as the spirit. Different cultures use different shapes and spirits. In some cultures, round masks represent celestial divinities and square terrestrial, and triangular ones from the underworld. The masks focus, but they open out into complex cosmological ideas.

F: "Some of the masks are much smaller or larger than the human face. Unsuitable for wearing. The bright feather mask of a parrot or sound mask of a finch."

S: "Yes. On some funerary poles in Nepal and Borneo, the soul of the deceased is transformed into a bird or plant."

F: "The fact of wearing masks displays the desire to produce an altered reality."

M: "Stop ganging up on me! We really don't see that in modern society anyway."

S: "Oh? What about horses, cars, spouses, clothes, titles, professions, jewelry, make-up, hair-dos, hats, tats, and spats? All ways to project an image or identity. These are not born with us. We make them as we live. We determine some of the reality with these masks, metaphorically. Like Herr Dr. Prof. Mirthless here. Is your title stitched on your pjs?"

M: "I don't see—well, no."

S: "Can I see them? Just kidding. These virtual masks are not so different from 'primitive' masks. They confer special powers and authority, don't they professor? When you wear the professor mask with bow tie, herring-bone jacket with leather elbow patches, and pipe, like now, you become endowed with certain magical powers, such as deciding failure or success, maybe even initiating the young girls into the mysteries of delicate elderly copulation rituals. Yet, when you go home, you take off the mask and cook beans and coffee. The masks are an integral part of our collective culture, and always have been and still are."

M: "How rude of you, my role is permanent. I have tenure. I eat pate faux gras with my tie on. I will not be dismissed or cowed by someone who still believes in ghosts and coyotes."

S: "But, the mask is part of your daily life now. Perhaps you *cannot* remove it anymore. How sad. Masks used to be removed and time given to grow out of the masked role. So you could be freed from power and live an ordinary life during the day. Your actions are rites as much as any 'primitive' ones. The masks have changed as we have become more agrarian and urban. They reflect astronauts and computers now, as well as birds and animals. But, if you want to see if these old masks are any less effective, just give animals masks to children!"

M: "That's meaningless. Children are immature adults. They grow out of fantasy when they become adults."

S: "How sad to think that the shrunken aged shell is more important than the expanding young consciousness."

F: "Masks reflect our dualism, psychological and cultural."

S: "Think of how the Iroquois people, my people, celebrated Memory Festivals that commemorated the migration of people from further north, or from Asia or Africa. That departure from the first paradise is the first great adventure of any people. And, the people took their customs and knowledge, their art and masks, with them."

M: "Yea? My people, the English, just celebrated achieving controlled nuclear fusion. And, they did it by throwing off the baggage of the past. What have you done recently?"

S: "Survived your people, and tried to teach you to live with joy and acceptance, and with understanding, by keeping our memories— and not surrendering to the nasty ways of the machines that you worship so uncritically!"

M: "Yea, well, my people are the ones leading—"

F: "Please! I'm not sure how important it is to compete, or to lead or to be noble. Let's sum up. One sentence each. Ms. Sheauga?"

S: "Coyote is a legend of Native Americans, whose lessons could be learned by all, even through questionable extension into the modern environment, since he is the ultimate survivor."

M: "It's amusing, like Beaver and Butthead, like a Saturday morning cartoon, good for keeping the kids out of the workshop or office."

S: "That's your problem. The kids need to learn things in the office and workshop. You separate them and they become irrelevant—"

M: "Not so! Kids are—"

F: "Thank you, both of you. Coyote, in this incarnation, is a mirror in which we can see nonsense and foolishness, or great meaning and identity. Please, look first, then decide."

Section Faces

Water Babies Or That Sinking Feeling

Realizing he was being followed through the grasses
by some invisible menace
Coyote dove into the pond. As he sank
in the clear water, Coyote stopped digesting
the mouse he had just snarfed up,
slowed his heart and focused on a water mote.
    The small molecules in his blood dumped
their oxygen into muscle tissues for later.
His heart kept beating, palunk, palunk, palluunk, paallluuunk
but slowed as he came to rest on the bottom.

Twenty feet away, under water, Wakanda watched;
she counted slowly to 1200, almost 20 minutes.
She knew she could wait and he would die
and that later, eventually, Fox would restore him
but she also knew that might take a lot of time.
    She knew she could save him, but then he would know
how much she loved his cheating, moth-eaten hide.
She stopped hesitating and thinking and pulled him up.

Coyote could feel a familiar touch but he could not see her
and his eyes were as open as a dead body's.
He knew who it was, he knew he was truly loved
by his former mate
and when they surfaced he spit water at her direction
and saw the shape of the water over her invisible face.
        He gasped dramatically and exclaimed:
"Thank you, noble ghost for rescuing me
from certain death! How can I ever repay you?
A mouse? A quick hump in the field? A bucket
of chicken, or gold? —
        Wakanda gently took his mask off,
or rather the mask of her face that he had put on earlier.
Coyote watched as the mask became invisible,
Then Wakanda's face painted itself with the brush
strokes of single hairs, and she stood over him
dripping water on him.

"Coyota—Wakanda, so nice to see you! I was—"

        She walked away, up into the field and jumped
for a mouse. She made a real display of tossing
the mouse and recapturing it, mixing it with dandelions,
knowing how much Coyote liked tossed salad
and how hungry he must be.

'Damn!' thought Coyote, and followed her; he was hungry
after all. But, he had hoped to avoid
having to ingratiate himself.
   She must have watched him this morning, seen him fly
in with his eagle wings and defeat the forces
of military-industrial media again.
Then, he was saved in water. Water was always good for him.
It was his sign; he could never fail in water.

She knew that he thought that she had seen him
at the end of the battle, biting the leg of an unconscious soldier.
She was sure he still thought about that silver bitch Matawaka,
but she would never speak about it. She wondered
if he would follow her.
    He did. Lust was life, but food was food.

Wakanda paints her mask

"I want to go visit my family; besides, it would be a good place to raise pups," Wakanda suggested.

"Oh, sure. Where is it?"

"Just east of here a bit."

"Oh, Montana?"

"No, Kansas."

"Kansas! That's almost on the east coast. How will we get there? Where there? Is it flat?"

"Buffalo are there. You like Buffalo, don't you?" Coyote started drooling at the idea of a buffalo dinner. "Okay, I guess, if you think so. I just have been away from Tucson for so long. I've been here, in Spokane, for over a year now."

"We can go south later, to see your family."

"Ah, sure," said Coyote, trying not to think of his family. "I thought you were Dakota? Your name I mean?" asked Coyote.

"I am, Dakota Sioux, the territory was larger than the new states. My name means 'magic power,' as you know."

"Yes, I remember," Coyote begrudged, remembering with envy that she knew several tricks he did not.

"I have a friend with the Kickapoo (Kiikaapoi) near Powhattan."

"Okay, as good a place as any. Is that near the Potawatomi?"

"Close. We can go there and make a wicki up."

They started walking the next day. At first Wakanda kept amusing him with stories of Kansas. "You know, Kansas is the Jayhawk state. Jayhawk is a mythical bird, red and blue, but immortal and invisible—"

"Then how can it be read and blue?"

"—able to change its size at will, becoming as large as a blimp—"

"Sounds like Moronhawk, over in the forest; got blimped up with some bad cow," Coyote commented. Wakanda was quiet, so Coyote knew he had to be respectful. "So, who came up with this name as flat as the land?"

Wakanda knew Coyote was trying to be good. "From a Dakota Sioux word, 'KaNze,' means south wind."

"Mmmm," said Coyote, "interesting."

Insincere as it was, Coyotes comment was enough to open the floodgates of his lonely mate, who said: "Kansas was called the Squatter state, because of the squatters who came over from the Slave state of Missouri, then it was the Grasshopper state, after

14

swarms of locusts. Then, the Sunflower state, cyclone state, wheat state, and center state."

"Not the Flat State? Is it all flat?" Coyote asked.
"No, it has hills in the west, well, higher plains. Good places for dens."

"Can we steal a car?" Coyote asked innocently.
"Not necessary. Tomorrow, after we have gone a bit further, we can put on masks and hitchhike."

"Oh, yea, I want the George Hamilton Mask!"
"No, you need something younger, I'll make a Mike Meyers mask."

"Who?"

The area looked like a giant grid cast over rolling hills. Coyote and Wakanda walked towards town, across Horned owl Road, then Kestrel Road, then Jackrabbit Road, and Kingfisher. "No Coyote Road," Coyote commented.

"No wolf or eagle, either," added Wakanda, "must be oriented to birds and cuddly vegetarians."
The first thing they noticed was the empty storefronts. Oh, that's right, everyone had moved to the big city for jobs. The people they did see looked poor, and there seemed to only be a few of them.
There was no Walmart, or Walgreen or Walstore or Walgrocery.
On the edge of town a buffalo loitered above some native grasses.
Coyote started to charge the buffalo, but Wakanda stood on his tail.

"What?" asked Coyote.

"Not yet, we don't know him yet," explained Wakanda. She spotted a good place on a small hill above town, "Start digging here."

"But, we're not facing the town—oh, yea, right."

She tried to teach him, or reteach him, his heritage, "Itsayaya, come here, please."

"No, never use that name again! Gods cannot have first names. It is demeaning. Imagine 'Joe God' or 'Nathan Yahweh.' Everyone would call him Nathan—Nathan, part this river, Nathan bring some rain—That's why—"

"Oh, what about Gautama Buddha?'
"Never mind, Just call me Coyote."

"Even in bed?"

"Okay, but whisper it, okay?"

After a long, lazy night, Coyote was eating left-over mouse scraps. Wakanda came over and spoke,

"Today, Octoye, we are going to learn how to become another animal without a mask. I want you to put on the mask of a, oh, a monkey."

"Okay, give me a minute," and Coyote bent over and made some confusing motions with ripping noises. A few minutes later he turned around and Wakanda screamed, "Woa! Who, what is that?"

"You can't tell? It's a baboon!"

"Oh, no," Wakanda walked around him and looked from the side. He had taped a banana peel on some cellophane and taped that to his face. It made his eyes look glassy. She noticed some packaging and a label that said, 'Masker Helper.' This was going to be harder than she thought. "Where did you get those other masks, You know, the George Hamilton mask?"

"Mail order, Masks B We.™"

"I think we have a lot to do."

"Okay, this wasn't too good on a moment's notice, but the rubber masks are quite good, with a little make-up, I haven't had any complaints."

"From whom would you have had complaints? Never mind. Here is how to start. I want you to imagine what it is like to be Badger. What does he look like? How does he walk? Can you become that?—take off the banana first!"

Coyote rolled his eyes back in his head. He hunched over and waddled away from her. But, his face and body did not change. Coyote knew that his mask was the interface between faces. He suspected it was something more for Wakanda, and he had to learn what.

"C'mere my Goosey Toocey," Wakanda invited.

Coyote came, but he was not happy with these pet names. Where did this one come from?

"I'll show you how to make a mask out of mist," she said.

"Can't we look for a buffalo first?"

"No, unless you want to try a buffalo mask now."

Coyote grunted and rolled by, trying to get into character, but remained a dog-like being.

Coyote started going out and studying the buffalo.
He noted that the one always near town was part of a private
herd of 60. The loner was grazing on grasses in the evening air.

Coyote approached him head-on.
Coyote looked up at Bison, whose light summer coat was turning
a dark brown for winter. Bison was 6 feet tall, 10 feet long and
weighed over 2000 pounds. His front half was massive,
with a delicate rear end. Coyote wondered if he had had
genetic work done. He shouted, "Hey, yo, grass-eater!
What shall we do today, play hunter and hunted?"

Suddenly the bison toppled over and started wallowing
in the dust. He snorted and looked over at Coyote, at eye-level, now.
"You're too small for a wolf. Who are you?"

Coyote replied, "You're too big for your brain. I Coyote
am hunting you."

Bison knew that even wolf packs would hunt only
small calves and almost never a healthy bull; maybe this little wolf
was daft. He looked at Coyote, noting that he was not displaying any
hunting behaviors, "Let me know when you're ready to begin, so I can
get a good head start, maybe 6 or 7 inches, okay?"

Coyote was too busy to answer, planning what part of Buffalo
to eat first; he was staring at the hatched area in back of the neck,
where the most tender meat was—the skin was not thick but the hair
mat was tremendous.

Then Bison stood and Coyote had to look up.
"Didn't there used to be more of you Buffalo?" Coyote asked
innocently.

Bison snorted dust, before answering, "Bison, not buffalo;
buffalo are big water cows. There were 83 and a half million of us, but
that was after humans got too sick and thin to hunt us."

"Okay, I'm ready," and Coyote charged.
But, Bison made a half turn and Coyote bounced off the massive head
and lay in the dust, watching clouds spin around him.
"I can't decide to trample you or talk with you," mused Bison.

"Umm, maybe we could talk. What do you taste like? Could
I have a quick bite, just a little?"

Bison snorted.
Coyote blew away a dust cloud and said, "Okay, glad that's settled.
How come you're by yourself?"

"I need room to think," ruminated Bison.

Coyote wanted to get closer to his new friend. He was always grazing near him, and in truth the grass settled his stomach, in small amounts.
Then, he found an old bleached buffalo skull.
He played with it, but soon got his head stuck in it.
Suddenly he heard thunder, but could not see any clouds.
Through an eye hole, he saw Bison charging him. He ran to a tree and jumped up as Bison hit the tree and it shook.

Coyote said, "Please don't kill me. I'm just an innocent whose head is stuck."

Bison said "Come down."
Coyote said, "Okay. Just one smoke and I can be content to die."
Bison said "Okay."

"Can I light you one?" Coyote asked.
Bison snorted no.

Coyote was smoking looking down at the large horns.
"You know I could sharpen those weapons and shine them up."
When Coyote leaned over, the weight of the skull pulled him off the branch and he plummeted down and hit Bison, skull to skull.
The old skull shattered and Coyote bounced in front of Bison, who was shaking off the collision.

"Sure. Why not?" Bison said.

Coyote sharpened the horns and buffed them up, using cigarette ashes to blacken a few spots.

With his new horns, Bison collected some cows from the younger males unwilling to fight an old icon with shiny horns. He gave Coyote one cow as a favor, "Cut a little fat from her, then rub ashes in the wound and it will heal. You can eat forever."

That was great, but after a time Coyote wanted a little bone marrow and liver. He tricked her into resting, then killed her and skinned her, but then so many crows and magpies came that they ate the meat and all that was left was scraps.

Coyote went back to get another cow, but Bison said "No."
Coyote howled in frustration, "Ai-oo, ai-oo, ai-OO!"

Months later, Coyote saw Bison and hailed him, "Hey, thunderhead, what shall we play today?"

Bison was chewing, "We could have a race."
Just what Coyote had planned. Coyote jumped into a lead quickly

by racing ahead, then tripping, and pretending to fall hard.
As Bison thundered by, Coyote leaped up and raced around to the bottom of the steppe, where he looked for the mangled buffalo, who should have fallen off the edge by then. He heard a rumbling sound and looked up as something heavy plummeted towards him.

He barely avoided being crushed by a boulder.
Then he saw Buffalo's big head looking over the edge.

"Are you okay, little headbutter?"
Coyote nodded but was working on another plan for his gigantic thanksgiving meal.

Bison skull

Coyote Goes to High School

Wakanda watched Coyote as he played with his wrist
then lay down, bowed to the northwest,
placed his paws flat and stayed in that position,
looking at his wrist.
 Finally, Wakanda could not be quiet any longer:
"What are you doing? Praying to Mecca?
That's the wrong direction."
   Coyote sat up and looked at his wrist,
"It still has the wrong time!"
Wakanda noticed the shiny watch for the first time.
 Coyote continued, "The directions said
to put the watch on a nonmetal surface facing
Colorado so it could pick up the atomic signal.
It doesn't work."
    "Oh, you weren't praying?"
 "No, it was technical."
     Wakanda wondered if technology
required the same physical distortions as religion.

"Look, my lovely 'cootey,' we need to get some food,"
Wakanda said affectionately.
    "Kootie? Where do you get
these names for me? Why do you call me that?"
 "They're anagrams of Coyote. You're my cool
Ecotoy, baby!"
   "What's an amagran?"
     "Oh, you poor puppy. I forgot,
you dropped out of predator school. Did you ever learn to read?"
 "Sure, I can read. Need I remind you that I have been a lawyer
and a professor."
   "Of course, but I thought you made up the diplomas
and things. Why don't you go to school for real?"
 Coyote hated it when she spoke down to him. He knew in his
heart that he did not need more education and he did not want to go
to amagrand city just to learn a few silly skills or theories.
He sulked, until she called:
     "Yo-Teco! Let's have some fun in the field!"
Coyote knew her code words for sex—all he had to do was agree
to some form of social torture.

She made arrangements with the local humans and suddenly
he was going school.

"I'm sure glad we're not going to that prison
over there," Coyote said as he approached the one-story building in
light turquoise in front of him.
"We are," said the boy next to him,
"that is the high school, this is the security building checkpoint."
Then, Coyote was separated and put on a conveyor belt through
beeping and blinking electronic columns.
"Sir, please remove your backpack and put it on the table."
Coyote was frisked after being x-rayed.

Coyote asked his new friend, "Where are the lockers?"
"Lockers? Where have you been? The Ads got rid of them,
saying they were just hidey holes for weapons and drugs."
"What do I do with my books and coat?"
"Carry them with you at all times."
"Is there still a lunch room?"
"Follow me."
At first, it looked like a normal lunch room, but then
Coyote noticed that there was no counter, no food. His new friend,
Cobbler, a friend of proximity, pointed to the far wall.
Coyote saw the banks of windowed food, like mail boxes or Horn &
Hardart's in New York. Each slot had something and the slots were
arranged by fruits, vegetables, wrapped cold meats, cheeses, and fluids.

Then it was time for orientation. A pretty bubbly girl addressed
the new students. For some reason she reminded Coyote of
Hummingbird.
"Here's orientation: Got'yer Bullet-proof vests?
Gas masks? Just kidding, ha, ha."
Her voice was so squeaky, Coyote rubbed his ears.
"So what's high school really like? Is it more work? More stress? Do
you want to kill the older students? Burn down the school? Shoot
yourself? If you're having thoughts like these, you're not alone: Lots
of other freshmen are feeling the same way you are! But, don't decide,
yet!" And Amber paused.
"Here are a few topics that commonly worry
incoming freshmen and some things you might want to know about
them. You may not know a lot of people when you start high school.

You may feel like fresh meat in an assassin supermarket. Talk to your neighbors, and you'll probably find that a lot of them are feeling just like you are. They're all new to the school and don't know *what* to expect." Amber paused again to adjust her skirt and pull down something underneath.

"The workload will be harder here as you get more advanced knowledge of many academic subjects. So you may find things more *challenging*. If you ever find your work too overwhelming, teachers and tutors are available to help. Of course, high school also has more extracurriculars, such as clubs, music, theater groups, student government, and sports teams. This is a fantastic time to explore your interests and try new things. School does not have to be *all* work and no play. These activities may take place before or after school, or during free periods or study halls."

Coyote tuned out of the words as he noticed her hand around the hem of her skirt. Coyote realized right away what generations of students had realized—high school was day-care for teenagers, age segregation for suckers. Sit and stay until you're eighteen.

Amber was still orienteering: "High school is a time of increasing independence and responsibility. But if you ever find that personal issues get really overwhelming, find someone to talk to. You're not alone. Becoming more independent does not mean being alone. Friends and parents can be great resources, but sometimes that's not *enough*. School counselors or other therapists can be very helpful.

"High school gives you the chance to take off those training wheels and learn how to be more independent. It's perfectly okay if you're nervous at first. Everybody's a bit wobbly the first time they take off their training wheels. Just be patient and keep trying. Once you've adjusted to your new independence you may find you can go further than you ever *imagined*.

"Here are a few rules that I found work, a few dos and donts for being a successful freshperson. DO: Expect to be treated like a freshman, *expect* to have upperclassmen push you around or beat you senseless, expect to be last in everything, try to make friends with other losers, work hard to get what you want, and be yourself! DON'T: Act like you *rule* the school, it will just make upperclassmen hate you even more; be afraid to talk to new people; skank it out to get upperclassmen guys to notice you; act tough or like you're better than the upperclassmen. Basically, know your *place*, and you'll be good. Now, go out there and have *fun*. The first day should be spent getting to your classes, meeting your teachers and peers, and participating in the social aspects of everything! Okay. Bye!"

Coyote noticed that his wallet was missing. Maybe he could track it by smell.

Coyote looked at the classes he had been assigned. He shuffled to them in order. Cobbler was like his shadow.

Coyote asked: "How come we are in the same classes?"

"We're freshmen, I-J. Hey, are you an Indian? Sioux? NezPerce? Itsayaya Jones. Wow, I didn't know."

Coyote tuned him out, still angry at Wakanda for the name thing. He looked at the course list: Shakespeare for simpletons, Math for dummies, History for idiots, and Ecology of headline news. Shakespeare in ebonics? The teacher was an old black woman with white hair. Coyote knew that anything could be improved so he decided to rewrite Shaky, since 'all the world's a stage' in evolution, as evidenced by Coyote himself.

History? An old white man who must have witnessed all of history. Forget the past, we can't repeat it if things get worse all the time. Better to reinvent the past to cut out the embarrassing mistakes.

Math for dummies; the prerequisite for this course was math for imbeciles, but Coyote could pretend. The teacher was a young woman, stylishly dressed, but acne had written her career choice on her face. All he had to do was use logic to make the teacher feel bad. "You gave me an F on this test. I am a hard-working, good Christian American patriot. What is it you hate most? God? America? Hard work? Certainly, you could change it to a 'Bush D' so I could run for president later, when I will have people to do the math for me and give me prompts."

Ecology and headline news. That was like a detective story, following clues. The first class was sort of interesting as the teacher, an ancient, balding guy with a beer belly started with the local recession and worked backwards through economic shifts to changes in agriculture, changes in culture, and changes in clothes. The teacher tried to relate that to genetics and history and cultures, but, mostly to make everyone do something necessary and important, only if it to study a pond to see why the native vegetation died. Hey, we can do that, Coyote thought.

Most of the kids were really working harder at popularity, studying
it and testing it like neurosurgeons preparing to be wealthy.
But, the standards for coolness were atmospheric, and few were going
to make it. Yet, all of them had the intrinsic cruelty to torture
the nerds at the bottom of the pecking order. This created a target
for the rage of failure. Woa, just like politics, Coyote realized.

"Yes, warden, I mean, teacher." Coyote said, as he was asked to move
along to his next class. School was a little world, a microcosm, and
because it was little, there was no room to move and certainly no way
to escape.

"Well, that's because kids have no active role, no meaningful
position in urban industrial society. Not like when we were farmers or
hunters," Cobbler said cleverly.

"Not so, we can be fast food minions
and rule the world," Coyote replied. How come he didn't get stuck
with a cute popular girl as his first sudden friend?

"No, the world is ruled by glandular giants, tossing a ball over
or through something, as if it were the most important thing of all,
and being rewarded as if it were! These turds rise to the top and get
more rewards,"

"That's because we make the hierarchy before any
of us has more than just basic motor skills," Coyote noted.

"Okay, and it becomes a popularity contest, and it always is,
speaking of which," they had arrived at the end of the hall, where
popular girls held court.

"No, high school is like a musical," said Trina
the happy cheerleader. "I just can't wait to sing about life. Maybe I
should be a singer not a gymnast?"

A Stepford Student, Coyote thought.
Then, Coyote ducked a slow fist.

"Hey, you was drooling over my girl!"
Coyote bit a cauliflower ear.

A large heavyset teacher shouted, "Hey!"
and stood between them. There was lot of name-calling and bullying,
a little blood and torn shirts.

Someone shouted, "Get 'em, coach!"
Coyote moved aside and sashayed out of range.

Hey, high school was really just like politics!

Coyote established himself as an alpha male by biting or fouling anyone who tried to bully or mock him. However, most of the girls ignored him as he was not tall or bulked up. Except for one young woman who came up and stroked his haunch.

"Hi, sailor, I'm Fifi Yoplait," she introduced herself.

"French?" Coyote asked.

"Yes!" and she grabbed his muzzle and dragged him to a closet.

Hours later Coyote felt like talking, "So, is that a normal French greeting?"

"No, only to legends. Say, why is your penis all scarred up like that? Is that part of some secret Aztec ritual?"

"Yes," Coyote lied, not wanting to admit that the experiment with the boojum shaft penis extender had been a painful failure. It had taken days to dry it out and work it off. But, for a while he had the largest shaft on the planet. "It marks me as a special warrior who fights without fighting."

"Fight without fighting? That sounds awfully Bruce Lee, philosophically speaking. Does that mean you win without winning?"

"No, there is never a winner to violence. That is why I am a wise man and a lover."

"Oh, do you love without making love, too?"

"I have not mastered that, although I can lick—"

"No, doggie style, Loupie!"

"Hey, wait, I don—woof!"

So this was high school!

Coyote dragged his book-laden pack home, his ripped clothes hanging loose. Wakanda just shook her head and nodded towards a stale mouse salad.

Badger came close to Rabbit, who was busy eating his own dung. "That is gross? Why do you do that?"

Rabbit looked up, chewing thoughtfully, "I need to recover the vitamins."

"What vitamins?"

"B12"

"I thought that was an old bomber?"

"No, vitamin."

"Can't you eat it or make it?"

"Not enough bacteria in my gut. I would have to eat meat or eggs."

"How do you know that? Well, I don't have to eat mine."

"No, because you eat meat and your gut is longer. Discovery channel. Here taste this."

"No thanks. I've seen Mouse do it. You're just a giant mouse," said Badger.

"No, not so!" said Rabbit, "we proud rabbits are more closely related to primates. Just look at the molecular form of some of our proteins!"

"How do you know that? You can't read."

"Discovery channel."

"Where? Hey, I just thought of something. Coyote eats meat *and* he eats his own dung. Why does he do that?"

"No reason—maybe he just likes it?" Rabbit guessed.

"Where is ol' yellow eyes?" Badger asked.

Coyote was working on a totally new, awesome mask, a scary mask, something with more teeth than a lamprey or wolf, something more threatening than a coiled snake. In fact, nothing but teeth.
He looked at bird's beaks, and—then, he had it. He started looking through the faculty parking lot. The faces of cars were oddly animal-like, yet metallic and unkillable. Then he saw the grill of a 58 Plymouth, even the name suggested devouring. But, no, too whale-like with that metal baleen. Most of the new cars looked like lamprey eels or funny otters. Then he saw a 1950 Buick with giant chrome teeth, like a deranged bucktooth saber-tooth tiger. The two bright eyes, the high round nose, the metal teeth. A fright mask to scare the uninitiated enemies. He was able to build one from scrap and few stolen items. Now, to find someone to scare.

Coyote slowly turned his nose into the wind. The bulbs inside lit up. He could read the entire flow; someone was rotting, someone else was being born. The Minks had quarreled. Rabbit was sneaking around the tree out of sight. The smell of Rabbit reminded him of a thousand earlier meals. He put on the metal mask. The smells the memories— this is how Coyote had started to think, to wonder. Then, everything else was forgotten as he chased the smell of a turkey.

"You should have seen me," Coyote was saying, "He fought, clawed me, pecked me, twisted this way and that, and I hung on to his scrawny neck and bit and chewed and clamped and held, then he died. Feathers everywhere, blood everywhere, some of it mine, but I stood over his body and howled in triumph, me Coyote."

Wakanda looked up and asked, "What was his name?"
"Name?"

"Yes, did he have a name?"

"Well, duh, dogmeat, or maybe deadmeat, huh," Coyote shrugged.

"Don't you think you should have asked his name so you could pay respect before you killed him?"

"Killed him? This was a battle of the ages. I won a war," Coyote was getting miffed.

"Yes, but we should always ask first and always be thankful afterwards."

Coyote hung his head down then up, trying to make it look like agreement, "Yes, of course, I will ask next time, but just before I close, so he can't get away while I am following these nice formalities. Okay?"

"I just wanted to know who we were eating. He sure is juicy, If we knew who he was we could find a few relatives and not have so many dry, scrawny birds."

Coyote took this to be a criticism also, "Dry birds? Do you know—"

After dinner, Coyote wanted to mate, "It's all about connectivity." Wakanda recognized that third-person perspective and boffed his head. "You are Itsayaya, stop distancing from me. Start prancing for fun in the field, Tecoyo."

That evening the pups were conceived.

Coyote was hungry, again. That was not unusual. But, he couldn't find
any mice. That was unusual. Where were all the mice? Mice had to be
everywhere. Every acre was home to tons of mice. They just were not
here. Nor did he see any prairie dogs or ground squirrels.

Coyote looked for Vulture. No vultures circling, so no dead deer.
He looked for Crow. No crows, so, no dead porcupines. He looked
over the Kansas fields. Nothing but grain, hill after hill.
Should be mice, a lot of mice.

He dug a small test hole. Nothing.
This was really perplexing. Where in the hell did all the mice go?

He saw a solitary crow and followed him, as the crow flew east into
Powhattan. Coyote had to slink along the streets, from Third street to
Fourth street from dumpster to dumpster. This was not a good part of
town. He suspected coyotes had been shot in this area. Not because
they were being hunted and eliminated as pests, but because the local
gangs loved to practice their marksmanship on dogs and coyotes.

Crow landed on a two-story brick building, looked around and flew
down into the alley.

Coyote lost sight of him, but smelled a faint
whiff of roasted meat, tantalizing because he could not
identify the kind. Well, this was new.
Coyote had tried a lot of different animals,
so he should know it. Maybe the cooking and spices
were fooling his snozzer. No, not possible.
This was a nose that could isolate, categorize
and contain any smell.

He jumped in a dumpster and looked for some
materials. With some coffee grounds and styrofoam
he made a Chris Rock mask.

The sign over the alley spelled "Chez Sapience."
Coyote watched a few people go in, including one tall
man with a tattooed face. He followed shortly.
He was asked at the top of the stairs if he had
a reservation. "Yes," he answered, "I am with Crow,"

knowing that crow had eaten everything at one time.

But, then he was let in and led to a table where a large black man sat, looking like Cedric the Explainer. "Crow, it is you?"

"Of course, and I knew you would find this place eventually."

"Why, what's so great about it?"

"It serves many kinds of food. I come for the long pig."

"What?"

"Human meat. It's good, it tastes like wild pig." The waiter came back, so they both ordered.

Coyote said "No, tastes more like possum. Where does it come from?"

"Road kill, most likely, car-over-cliff kind of thing, not found for months. Although I hear Fox actually hunts them live."

"Oh, no," Coyote groaned, wondering where Fox was.

"I like eating rare species," Crow mentioned between mouthfuls.

"But, humans aren't rare!"

"So what? Then, it's more like eating beautiful species." "But, humans aren't beautiful!"

"Then it's more like eating an intelligent species like an elephant or a dolphin, or crow."

"But, humans aren't intelligent!" Coyote protested, "They cannot stop killing themselves or other species. They cannot stop doing anything, as long as it is sweet or fun."

"You're right. I give up. We should eat them because they are dead, recently freshly dead, I mean."

"But, eating them should be taboo," insisted Coyote.

"Like eating coyote or crow?" asked Crow. "This is great! Here we can rest, and eat, all watched over by carnivores of loving grace."

Coyote coughed up a piece of meat, and put it on his plate, unsure of what to do next. Maybe it was good, maybe it would have been better cooked.

Crow stood up and said, "I'm going to dance? Coming?"

Coyote got home late and went to sleep by his mate, who did not wake up. He dreamed of fleas eating him as he slept. Early the next morning, he told Wakanda he had to get to a seminar.

"Coyote, that's the herbivore's seminar. You can't go to that— you're not a herbivore."

"Don't worry, I'm just going to the lunch."

Coyote knew the blessed day was coming by the change
in his mate's diet, the constant cravings for hard-to-find foods,
like violets or bats.

He lay outside the den, rolling over at every small
groan; he did not understand why she wanted to have pups
the traditional way, in a hole in the ground, although he had
to admit that the soil was good for digging. Then it was quiet.
He crawled down the entrance.

"Six pups, that's great!"

"Seven,"

"What, I don't see seven?"

Wakanda held her paws apart and close to Coyote's muzzle—
then he felt a wet tongue lick the corner of his mouth,

"Oh, no, it's invisible. No. No! Make it appear."
Wakanda licked the pup's face and an outline slowly
appeared. Coyote sighed.

"I'm going to call her Uzume. Do you
have names for your three?"

"Uzume, I remember that name.
The Japanese dancer, right? Yes, of course I'm ready. I'm going to call
mine Topkan, Skhelep and Napetym."

"Nappitime?"

"It's a Navajo name for 'First angry.' I got it from Moronhawk
and you know how smart he is. What names did you decide on?"

"Xegwe, Yoniatario, Zora."

"Zora? What kind of name is that?"

"It means 'dawn.' Did you notice the name order?"

"Yea, naturally."

"These are my last pups, last litter."

"I may not want to stop, you know. Pups are easy and they worship
me," Coyote said, although he was secretly relieved; there were such
risks with children, and even success was attended by stress
and strife—failure was worse. He knew he himself was stuck
at stage 3 of the grieving process, 'bargaining,' and he never got
to depression or acceptance—more bargaining was always possible.
He wondered how Wakanda felt about the loss of so many of her
pups, especially the loss of Denny at Dizzyland from overeating.
He had seen her sometimes looking west towards the setting sun.

Then he felt a pulling and saw one of the pups trying to suckle on his stomach hairs. He grabbed it by the scruff and held it up, "Which one is this?" he asked and moved it under Wakanda, who closed her eyes and lay back.

"That was Topkan; he likes you."

Ah, parenthood. He wondered how this litter was going to turn out. He brought in a few dead mice, then headed out for a walk. He knew the pups would be boring little tubs for the next few weeks, so, except for bringing daily food, he was going to be scarce.

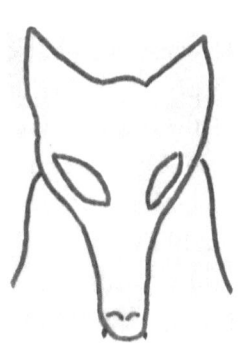

Wakanda's coyote mask

Coyote went down to Hazel Creek and watched for Otter,
who had followed them from Washington state. Coyote
thought that was real loyalty. He snoozed until he heard splashing.
He rolled over and looked at his friend sliding into the water.
"Are you married, Musty?"

"Lonny, it's Lonny. Married? I'm an animal.
Mates come and go," answered Otter, floating on his back and playing
with a pebble on his chest.

"Not necessarily. Some mate for life."

"Maybe, but if you refer to Wolf, Mrs. Wolf is getting poled on
the side pretty regularly by Gamma."

"So?"

"No, there's no Mrs. Otter."

"Why not?"

"I can't find anyone."

"What do you mean?"

"There are no female otters that I can find. They all disappeared."

Coyote mulled this over. He wanted to help his friend, who had
always been loyal and worshipful, like a friend should be—
then he remembered that Otter did not have to go to high school—
then he remembered the times Otter had helped him.
Maybe he could get payback by having Otter go with him to High
School if he could find a suitable warm body for his buddy.
So, he would help Otter, and he thought he knew how.

"I think, they're all in prison, Musty, but I know where that is."

"It's Lonny. Prison? Do you suppose they are evil
and dangerous?"

"I like that in a woman," Coyote said. "Let's scope
them out. It's a couple dinners down the road in FarmerBrownVille.
C'mon, roadtrip."

Otter did not really like road trips, due to his length-
challenged legs. He would have preferred water sledding, but now
he was intrigued by how smart Coyote was, to know where to find
mates—Coyote could find something to mate with anywhere.

It was getting dark, when Otter heard Coyote say, "We're here."
All Otter could see was a line of trees nearby.

"On the other side

of the trees is a wall, and on the other side of that is warm otter—"
Otter was running towards the wall, past a sign that said 'Zoo,'
when Coyote tackled him. Otter bit him out of irritation,
but Coyote only quieted him, "We have to sneak in, unnoticed.
Just follow me around this winding road."

Otter was amazed. There were many kinds of animals he had never
seen before, a few with huge teeth and claws, and only 2 or 3 of
each. But, his nose made him brave and lead him to a concrete
waterway with a cave and an elevated wooden house. The source of
the delightful scent was in the house. Otter started to race there, but
Coyote kicked him in the water.
      "Wait! You cannot get through the fence. We can climb this tree
and I will lower you down with a rope, okay? Okay!?"
      Lonny was salivating freely, so Coyote guided him to the tree.
When Otter jumped, Coyote lost his grip and fell.
      For a second, he was worried that he would crush Otter,
but Otter was flying to his destiny, and Coyote hit hard on the rocks.

Coyote lay there until dawn, trying to breathe without pain.
                              Finally Lonny came out and lay down.
"Whew! I had almost forgotten what that was like, the flood
of the senses, hurricane of emotion, the volcano—"
                                          "Yea. Mine are
flooding, too. Can we go?"
                        "Maybe just a few weeks, maybe, huh?"
   "Now! I think we can get up the tree if—" then Coyote saw the rope
was out of reach. Coyote spoke to Otter, who lured out his new love.
      Coyote went in and hid during the day wrapping his tail tightly
across his nose. After three days, Coyote hatched a plan.
      He worked to make a Voldemort mask out of a rubber mat.
When Randi and Joan came to feed the otters, a new zookeeper
was waiting with a string around Otter's neck.
                                    "Sorry M'am, just
finished breeding them. Gotta take this little guy back to Cincinnati
zoo. Pardon me."
                  "How did you get in? Who are you? What zoo?"
                     "Not important. All done, Scuse me,"
and he ran to the exit carrying a struggling Otter.

Outside, they were on a street with houses on both sides.
Coyote told Otter, "We are trapped. There is nowhere to go.
No escape from anything. No territory for the pups now.
Humans have divided it all up and spirit help us if we stray
from the boundaries we are allocated."

On the other hand, Coyote
loved suburbia. Food was much closer than it was in the wilds
and much dumber. Maybe this was the new wilderness
that he had dreamed of. Some of those little dogs barked at you
right up until you gobbled them down. Suburbia was a new
entitlement for Coyote. It was his inalienable right to have slow,
stupid, fat food.

Otter started wandering back to the zoo,
as Coyote looked for a fat little dog of some kind.

Coyote had to train the family. It was going to be harder
than he thought. Two of the pups had inherited their mother's ability
to form masks almost automatically, wherever they were. Coyote could
not do that, so his envy was tempered by fear. And, the others seemed
comfortable with his old rubber human masks. So, after he showed
them to always piss down wind, and away from the den, then
he had to show them how to do the same things as humans.

"First of all kids, you cannot piss anywhere; you have to travel to a
special room."
                    "Is that because it's so valuable?" asked Topkan.
"No, just the opposite? Humans try to be anonymous, shit-wise."
                    "Then how do they communicate?" asked Xegwe.
    "Yea, how do they tell who is sick or where they are going?" added
Napptym.
                    "It's all noise. They talk and honk." explained Coyote, "Now,
pay attention: In human shape, you find these rooms, usually white
and down long hallways—"
                    "What's a hallway?" asked Zora, the slow one.
"You didn't listen yesterday, did you?"
                                        "Huh-uh."
    "Okay, hallways are closed trails between dens. Now, once you find
this room, you have to take off your clothing and sit on a hollow stone.
Then poop. Then clean yourself with paper—"
    "Where does that come from?" asked Skhelep, the most like Coyote.
"Let's take a field trip." Coyote suggested, leading the pups into town.

Later, in the Uniontown Mall.
"Okay, Skhelep, good. Now put the paper in the hole, or in that other
hole over—No!" screamed Coyote.
                                "What's wrong?"
    "You wiped your nose with it afterwards. It's on your nose."
                        "So, I can lick it off."
"What do we do with the clothes? Put them in a hole?" Xegwe asked.
                "No, back on. You can't go naked."
"But, how will others know if we are interested in them,
I mean, really interested?" Topkan asked.
                                "Noise again."
"So, we have to hide our fur under artificial fur?"

"Yes. Now, you have to water your dung."
"But, I already watered it!"
"No, with clean water from the other hole. Press that metal thing."
"Can I drink it first?"
"No, there are separate places to drink."
"It's called input and output, dad," Skhelep suggested.
"Yes, well, in general, yes."
"Can we sleep there?"
"No, has to be that other den, where you keep your human clothes.
And, you can't just eat anywhere either, only in special rooms."
"You mean we have to kill a mouse and carry it to another room?"
"No, you cannot kill mice at all in human form. You have to let others
kill the mice and bring them—"
"To us?"
"No, to a special room for fixing. Then you buy them there—
"With what?"
"Good question. With a special kind of dung, or symbol. Say you take
a stick over—the stick represents old food, no, I mean, any food."
Coyote seriously wondered how humans trained their young.
"Okay, we can't communicate with scent. How do we?" asked Xegwe.
"Just low growling, using words."
"No howling?"
"No, never, unless you are in pain. It upsets people and scares them."
"So, it's not like that horn thing you mentioned."
"No, only machines are allowed to be loud."

Back home, Coyote continued his instruction.
Coyote wanted the pups to have fun as they grew up, so he took
it upon himself to teach them how to hunt and then
how to eat. "Don't **not** play with your food! Com'on, **play**.
Throw it in the air and push it in the dirt."
The pups were sitting and eating politely.
"Hey, stop that! Chew with your mouth open. And, you, leave more
food on your plate. There are starving crows that need to eat also; leave
them something."
"Is that why they always come late to dinner?"
"Yes, dear, it's just good manners," added Wakanda, quite happy with
Coyote's work.

That night Coyote put the pups to bed. "What is that?" Coyote asked
suspiciously.

Topkan rolled over on some crinkly papers.
Coyote nosed him over and pulled out a yellow paper
that said 'McDucks.' "How did, where did you get this?"

"I bought it dad. Some of us went on a field trip.
It was really good. Can we go back soon, huh? Huh?"

Four of the other
pups woke up and repeated the refrain, "Huh? Huh?"

"We want happy meals at the happiest place on earth!"
Topkan shouted.

Coyote wondered if brand loyalty began at two
months. These little monsters were insistent.

But, Coyote was prouder of these pups than any he had before.
He even put a bumpersticker on his stolen mustang:

"My cub is a star predator at Grassland Elementary School"
Close enough, though he was mildly surprised that none of the
stickers were printed for pups.

Now, they wanted to join something called 'Pupscouts.'

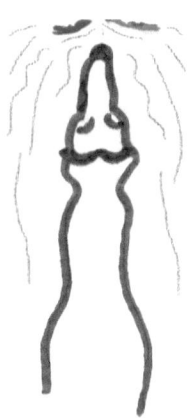

Coyote navigates the sea of smells

Wakanda was ready for a night out, but Coyote had no idea
that she wanted human culture this time. She suggested a night
at the opera.

Coyote accepted this penalty night gracefully (he thought).
Wakanda was thrilled, and made him wear his formal Vincent
Price mask.

They ran to a nearby bus stop and changed for the evening.
Three buses, two towns and three hours later, they were in the city,
Wichita, near a smallish building with lights.

They were led to a box with another couple. Coyote nodded at the
male, who looked like Beaver, as Wakanda was gracious to the woman.
An usher helped them be seated. Coyote sniffed his hand afterwards.
As Coyote sat there, he made a canny analysis of the performance:
A fat girl in a white dress sits on a wooden wall. A man in tight
white silk tights, over a tighter whiter girdle, sings and waves his arms
around, causing her to sing, also. Then they sing together louder
and louder. Then she goes away and another man comes out
and forces him to sing with him. Apparently, the purpose of the opera
was to promote singing with others in costumes.

"Who is that handsome blonde man, in the girdle?" Wakanda asked
her new friend Eleanor.

"That's the famous Tenor, Engeldolph
Himmerdunck, isn't he a hunk?"

"Who is the woman singing with him?"
"That's Mikia Toshiko."

"It looks like someone I know, well," Wakanda
said, thinking of Uzume. "Now, who is singing bass?"

"That's Swietoslaw Przemysl, the famous Polish singer
on loan from the Portland Opera."

"They must train every waking moment."

"And then some. I hear Swietie has tapes that run all night.

Coyote tuned out the rest of the night, except for his reward
from Wakanda. Not what he expected, it was a signed program from
Engeldolph.

Defaced

The Commonwealth of Animal Nations

"Animal problems? Animal problems!??" Squeaked Bluejay.
"No! These are human problems—waste, warming, whatnot. Animals just go where they can survive. They take advantage of openings in the forest. The opening that the forest advertises. Look," Bluejay said, "Right here. Niche available for cedar tree worm eating specialist, right there in green and brown. I could do that but I prefer seeds from pinecones. But, some bird is going to come along and fit that address and position perfectly. Just wait and see."
"What are you saying?" asked Skunk.
"I forgot."
"Animals have no say anymore in converting things. The humans are taking all the power. We have to unite so that our power is equal and undeniable," urged Skunk.
The animals murmured.
"We need some principles to agree on," suggested Skunk.
"All animals are equal," suggested Bat.
"Well, obviously not," said bear, extending a claw under bat's flesh-flower nose.
"I don't mean equal in weight or intellect or senses," replied Bat, "but having the equal chance to sit at the table, so to speak, and eat."
Rabbit said to Bear, "Hey leave him alone. You're not so great."
"Oh? Yes?" said Bear.
"Yea, before you, there was a flat-faced bear that could run faster than Wolf and bring down giant elk."
"I didn't know that. How do you?"
"Discover channel," said Rabbit.
"How could anything be faster than me?" asked Wolf.
"You're not so big either. The older wolf, Direwolf, was bigger and faster than you."
"And, where is he now?"
"I guess with Sabertooth and Camel. I don't know. This continent is hard on animals," admitted Rabbit.
Snake became the voice of reason, suggesting that they talk to some humans and get help. "Get a voice for animals and plants

in the human sphere."

The animals all agreed with that.

"How shall we choose a speaker? What about the wisest, Owl?"

"How about the one who has survived the longest?" asked Mouse, "Wouldn't that be the wisest, also? I offer myself. I came from India about 900,000 years ago. As I remember, most of you, Wolf, Bison, and everyone came here about 13,000 years ago."

The meeting broke down with shouting as each animal proclaimed their long heritage and why they were wise.

Until termite spoke up: "One hundred twenty million years. Thank you, let me make a few suggestions about organizing. The Queen will represent all of us. Humans respect queens."

Oh, no, Coyote thought. He remembered her; she gave bad directions and was really negative. Coyote had tuned out the other animals as he was thinking.

Coyote thought he understood humanity. The clue was surplus. The first humans shared their collections and kills equally. But, when they started collecting grass seeds and had large surpluses, that they could store for long times, they immediately started spreading apart in possessions and wealth. And, their queer species started converting the land to grass pastures that fenced out everyone else. For animals to compete Coyote knew they had to acquire large surpluses. But, how? What could they collect that would not rot quickly? Things that humans could not eat? Land-territory? Would that start to make animals unequal? None were equal to Coyote, of course, so he felt no need to voice that truism.

Skunk closed the session, "We need to investigate more."

"Let's send Coyote, he can nose around and see what this new threat really is," said Turtle, "He's a sneaky little turd."

"Coyote is good," said Otter, "Why do you always belittle him?"

"Wait until he eats your mate," sighed Turtle.

Skunk pulled aside Otter and gave him a special assignment: To find a conservationist to attend the next meeting, preferably from Greenpeace.

Wakanda was cutting through the Tall grass prairie, when she saw a wolf cut towards her. She did the sensible thing and ran, but the wolf was faster. The wolf closed on Wakanda, but Wakanda broke right then broke left. When the wolf almost had her, she fell suddenly, tripping the larger wolf. Before the other could get up, Wakanda said, "Stop, you could kill me eventually, but you might be hurt and maybe break a leg. You would not want that."

Meoquanee was snarling but stopped, when she understood the truth of the coyote's words. She did not know how she had been tripped, but she did not want to risk injury just to teach a lesson.

Wakanda rolled over and left her throat exposed. Meoquanee closed her teeth gently on it and then lay down beside her, "Good run. I did not want to kill you, just chase you away from the good mice and good deer."

"I was just passing through to get food to my pups."

"How many?"

"Seven."

"Ah, a good number. I have three of my own. Odd numbers are best. What do you feed them?" Meoquanee asked.

"Mostly, mice, you?"

"Mice when I can. Deer when my mate Kahgegwagebow helps."

"Yes, why don't males get excited enough to help more?" Wakanda asked.

The sun came out and the two alpha females lay on the hill, discussing the strengths and weaknesses of their mates.

Further west, Coyote saw several small boys playing at war on the hill. He got on his stomach and wormed his way closer. Then they ran down the hill to a lodge, where girls were playing with dolls dressed in buckskin clothing. Coyote turned and slowly made his way down the hill, fitting his body to every bump and dip.
Then the boys and girls went inside to answer a call from their grandfather.

Coyote wriggled himself to the side of the lodge and was still. He heard the words of an elder inside.

"—see our warriors wear the skin of an otter. It is lucky.

It is big medicine no doubt. It came to pass in this way—"

Then a woman shouted and Coyote took off towards the trees.
No one chased him. He could not stop thinking about the power that
might come from an otter skin.

Coyote did not want Otter to sacrifice himself, but Coyote needed
the power from his fine coat. He was sure Otter would agree,
so he decided not to ask.

Coyote invented a council meeting, and then
stopped off to get Otter for it. It was a long way, and they stopped for
the night.

Coyote said, "I think we can stay here, but this is where it
rains fire sometimes. You sleep first and I'll stay awake. If it rains fire,
be sure to race to the river. Don't stop and get anything, okay?"

"Okay, thanks, I appreciate this," Otter said.
After Otter had hung up his coat and was asleep, Coyote took the
coals from the fire and went out side. He threw them into the air and
shouted, "Shit, it's raining fire! Run! Quick! Now!"

Otter raced out and jumped of the bluff into Plum Creek,
hitting a boulder on the edge. His furless, lifeless body drifted down
stream. Coyote took the coat and ran off.

"The body is basically just a tube with openings at both ends, crude
and high-maintenance. The legs are just to transport it to food.
The eyes to see food." Coyote opined.

"I am glad you came to me, Coyote.
Sit still and let me finish dressing you. Now then," Tepehkiiha said,
"I will make sure you succeed by getting you properly prepared."
She took out the black bison skin and decorated it with eagle feathers
at all four corners. This was his robe. She made a quiver of white
winter pine marten fur. Then, she made a medicine pouch of the black
otter skin. The moccasins were of black bear fur, and she made
a turban for him from black yarn and put Eagle feathers in it. She
gave him an ornamented pipe. This was to smoke. She painted him
perfectly and gave him a wampum necklace of eight strands.
He looked young and handsome, about the age one who was just old
enough to wear a breech cloth. When she was through, she almost fell
in love with him herself, but she knew better, much better.

There was a lot of grunting and yipping coming from the trees. Crow
glided up to a branch and looked at the grey shapes below. At first

he could not understand what they were doing. The noise was from wolves. The wolves were playing with a ball, maybe fourteen inches in diameter. One of the wolves ran with it, slapping it with a paw to make it go. Then, the ball moved to the side—by itself it seemed—until another wolf ran with it, pushing it forward with a wet nose. Then, the ball went sideways, as if it was alive. So, the ball would go side to side and the young wolves would push it forward, nosing it or slapping it with their paws. 'Wolf ball!' Crow thought.

Crow waited until Wolf was near the bounds of the game and spoke quietly of the death of Otter.
Wolf said, "Bring me the bones, and this once, just this once, I will bring him back to life."
Crow understood and brought back several bones to the forest. He told Wolf of his efforts to get the bones from the river.
Wolf listened as he ran three times in a circle around the bones. At the end of the last circle, he lay down and watched.
"Don't you have to speak some words?" Crow asked.
Wolf nosed the bones together, and the two of them watched as the bones stood and filled in.
With a sudden breath, Otter went, "Woof, oh, that hurt. What a fall? Is Coyote okay?"
Crow told him the story and Otter was sad, really sad.
"What will you do?" Crow asked him.
Otter did not answer.
"What will you do?" Crow asked Wolf.
"What someone should have done ages ago," Wolf said, and left.

Coyote was in the copse of trees trying to work his medicine to get power over some ghosts. He chanted and danced but no power came to him. He was beginning to doubt his Otter-skin bag, when Wolf came out of nowhere and grabbed his neck—that was Coyote's last image, of lips pulled back from big teeth. Wolf tore apart the carcass and scattered the remains, taking only the Otter skin with him.

The world was much bigger now and Fox had more ground to cover, and more duties to complete.
Coyote's spirit got antsy being dead, so he got in the Walnut creek and hung around the trout people for a long time. Finally, they relented and let him be a trout for a while. He

swam upstream with the rest, then he leapt out of the water and died. He had to wait for fox again.

Finally, Fox was passing through the stand of trees and saw a familiar clump of hairs. He automatically jumped over them and brought Coyote back to life.

"C'mon!" Coyote said, "I had to swim around for years. Try to get here sooner, would you?"

Fox looked at his brother and said, "I have project to work on." Now, Coyote was angry and curious. But, he said he had to do an Anger Dance first.

From high above, Vulture said, "Hey, I see ol' yellow-eyes is back."

"Yea, look at 'im singing up a storm. Notice he never moves when he sings. The dance is separate I guess. Then he goes waltzing across the grass after the song ends," said Hawk.

Fox takes a stand

The next day Fox caught himself a fat prairie dog, and after getting some embers properly glowing, he thrust the meat into the ashes and decided to take a nap while it roasted.

Coyote happened to pick up the scent of the meat and came over to investigate. Coyote wasted no time in eating the prairie dog meat off the bones. Then, he took some of the fat and rubbed it on Fox's lips, and ran off.

When Fox awoke, he found that his lips were greasy, and he thought to himself, 'That was good, but I don't remember eating it.' He saw the bones, so he was sure he had eaten it. But Fox was ravenously hungry, so he caught another and roasted it. He tried to stay awake, but he was weaker now and fell asleep. The same thing happened again. Now, Fox was suspicious. So, he caught a third one, but coated it in herbs from some plants. Then he pretended to sleep, but fell asleep for real.

Coyote came, ate, and smeared a little fat on Fox's lips. As he was leaving, he had tremendous cramps. He had to stop walking as his stomach churned and his rear end exploded.

When Fox woke up, he was able to locate Coyote by the smell, as well as the trail of dung, and the heavy tracks. "I thought that might be you. Why did you eat my special medicine?"

"Is that what it was? heh, heh," Coyote shrugged, "I wanted to make sure it was fresh enough for you. Can I help you catch another?"

Fox didn't answer. He was remembering how quiet it was when Coyote was dead. Maybe he should be slower next time. Coyote took the silence as a negative and ran off.

The next day, in the same grasslands, Coyote hailed Fox, who was poised above a mouse den, "Yo! Younger brother!"

Fox spoke softly, "Don't call me your brother, shifty."

"Come on, walk a way with me. Tell me of your family."

"They're dead, remember,"

"Oh, I meant, I thought you, ah, started a new one."

"No, I am dedicated to my work, now."

"That's good," Coyote said, feeling like a heel for forgetting the magnitude of Fox's tragedy. "What work is that?"

"I call it the Fox Underground Network," Fox said.

"Heh, heh heh, really?" asked Coyote.

"Yea, why?"

"Well, it's taken. It exists."

"Listen to tomorrow's headlines: Two chipmunks killed in hit and run on death road! A Fox expose of an unholy alliance: men and cows!"

"Should be effective, Coyote agreed, "Shall we hunt, now?" Coyote watched his graceful, slant-eyed friend, Fox, as he leapt, he rolled, he chased his tail, gradually disarming his prey with innocent play, but gradually drifting closer, until he pounced and captured the mouse. Coyote complimented Fox as a graceful dancer and an effective hunter, expecting to get a free mouse, but Fox ignored his pathetic whining.

"Don't piss there!" Fox shouted.

Startled, Coyote pissed all over his back foot. Cursing quietly, he asked Fox, "Why not?"

"Do you know where that goes?"

"Yea, into the ground."

"No, look how close to Pedee Creek you are. Some of that goes into the creek and down to the beaver dam, then on to the human's drinking water supply—hmmm, never mind," and Fox pissed directly into the creek.

"Hey maybe we could set up urinetracker on the computer," Coyote proposed, "and see where it really goes."

Fox thought he understood humanity. He understood why his family was murdered by humans. They were not as complex as he thought. He knew that basically humans wanted something for nothing. This base desire, the core component of their personalities, was what allowed industry to be replaced by entertainment. It was a chance to be someone else, more exciting and nicer looking, with more things and more room and more sexual partners. And, the biggest entertainment, gambling, which proved that some people got something for nothing, and therefore everyone could get something for nothing eventually if they waited and played. It was expected that they were entitled to something. The infection had distorted their very souls and made them weak, and this weakness made their financial and real estate bubbles inflate, and this made it possible for a clever animal to trick them, to con them out of the things they had. And, yet it had produced misery on a grand scale. As people became depressed, their architecture became depressed, from the grand or common architecture that allowed people to live

meaningful lives in comfort, to plain, dull buildings that sucked
the life out of them, that forced them to be alone and independent,
to spend everything to make patterns that destroyed them slowly,
after they were blinded to their fate. They were thoughtless to animals
and took their homes for race tracks and roads. The grand themes that
once wove them together had become silly theme parks that amused
them as they died. It had become a cartoon of life, except that they
would not be getting up again after the cartoon ended.

Coyote and Fox were walking in the western hills, talking about
Fox's latest plan for revenge. Fox had styled himself as an ecosystem
assassin now, a new job description, a new problem, a new kind of
terror—and all terrors can be traced back to the earth eventually, to
terra, that is.

   "I don't see any humans here," Coyote noted.
  Fox replied, "I understand humans better now than I did two
paragraphs ago. Notice their basic way of living. They are in fact
termites. They are born indoors, they live indoors, they die indoors.
Another indoors species, like termites! They work indoors, the get sick
indoors. Love, worship, play—all indoors. They only use the outside as
a corridor between ins. Wilderness is just a hallway to them."
   "Well, then, you'll have to learn to hunt indoors. Well, what
will you do?" Coyote asked.
     "Aim my bazooka—well, the one from Blango
Air Base—at any tower or building that has a smiley face on it!"
   "That's your solution? You think people will suddenly
become awake or conscious of their path if you blow up every
Wal-Mart and water tower around?"
      "I don't care. I'm happy to kill
them, until a few left wake up and change. I Fox promise this!"
   "You are insane now," Coyote noted, "because of your loss
I mean—not your fault, terrible tragedy."
  "So? I have a purpose, a lust to achieve something!"
       "Destruction?"
"No, education," Fox snapped, "about civicide and animicide."
  "You mean 'suicide'?"
    "No, this is a mass movement, not a couple
individual decisions."
   "Can we wrap this up and get a mouse or deer. I'm hungry."
Fox regarded his audience of one and spoke eloquently: "I have
a nightmare that animals will be sucked into the vortex of human

decline—look at beaver, for instance, who doesn't bother building a dam and a lodge anymore, just nibbling off the bottom of a Wal-Mart playhouse and moved it to the center of a puddle. That's sad. I have a nightmare, that nothing we do will stop the mad rush to destruction, that nothing they do will deter them from destroying everything. I have a nightmare that the earth cannot recover from everyone interfering with its cycles and draining down the capacity of renewal. I have a nightmare that we will make a desert planet too hot for any desert creature, and this from the image of the human desire for simplicity, the simplicity of extinction."

"I lost my appetite, where's the bazooka?" Coyote asked. Fox liked that about his friend, that his simple mind could be swayed by reason, or passion, or hunger.

Fox had found the scent of a hunter and used his sideways approach to get close enough to incapacitate the man with a simple bite to the balls, then the jugular.

"I call it Ecokill," explained Fox, standing over the warm body.

"I thought you were a vegan now?" asked Coyote.

"Yes, but I kill people and leave them for scavengers like Skunk and Eagle."

"I thought you liked meat?"

"I do, especially human."

"Any special persuasion?"

"Republicans. I find them much better marbled, although it is not as lean as the Greens or Democrats."

"Then why aren't you eating them?"

"Because, I want my cause to be pure."

"How can you do that?" Coyote asked.

"I got funding for my company, Insaneco."

"Can I be a supervisor?"

"Let's see. I have a new project here, trying to find some pests for corn. The food and water supplies are weak points of any civilization, regardless of its virtual virtuosity."

"I could be the supervisor," Coyote volunteered again, "in a perfectly efficient world, one person would do all the work and the rest of us would supervise or consume."

"Hypocrisy is one step towards change. You can be in charge of accounting," Fox conceded.

The lady in the dark blue cape was looking at the dream catchers in the houseboat store on the lake. She watched the proprietress come in, an attractive woman in her glowing middle-age, dressed in tan layers.

Ann asked the lady in blue, "Are you interested in one, the blue one?"

"No," said the woman and blew the catcher so it moved. Ann was sure she heard a faint moan from it, but she looked back at the woman, who was holding the deck of cards that Ann used. "Tell me about these animals please?"

"Do you want to buy the deck?"

"No, but I will reward your time," offered the woman in blue, who did not offer her name, which was Brigid.

Ann shrugged and took the cards, then laid out six at random.

Ann started: "Fox is a nocturnal canine, whose medicine is the ability to blend unnoticed into his surroundings. His hearing and other senses are acute. Fox is a hunter and survivor. His message to you is to playfully pursue your goals and objectives. Learn the art of camouflage to gain information from others undetected. Practice shape shifting to change your appearance or blend into the scenery. Learn to dance to improve your agility and increase stamina. Sniff people to test them before interacting with them; avoid those who smell wrong. Use humor to get what you want out of life."

"And, how would I get a message to him?"

Ann was confused, but decided to continue. "This card is Turtle. Turtle is a slow-moving reptile who loves water. He creates his shell from his ribs as he grows. He can hide in this shell when danger approaches. The medicine of Turtle is endurance and protection. Turtle's message to you is to slow down and move slowly to your goals. The race is not always to the swift. Connect with Mother Earth. Let her energy heal and comfort you. Trust your intuition. Turtle represents Goddess energy. What phase of your life are you in, now? Do you feel more like a Goddess or a Crone? Get in touch—oww, that hurts! Please let go." Ann could see her hand was turning white from the pressure of the other's hand.

The woman let go suddenly, and said, "Please continue."

"—in touch with your feelings, but remain grounded. Like turtle, you too have a protective shield, called an aura. I think yours needs some work to be stronger."

The woman ignored her comment and pointed to the last card on the left, "What is that medicine?"

"That is Badger. Badger is an aggressive nocturnal animal in the weasel family, who makes his home in an underground complex of burrows, called "earths," where he is knowledgeable of all of the healing roots of Mother Earth. Badger is the Medicine Chief and Keeper of Roots. Badger medicine is serious and the opposite of being passive. The badger claws can dig deep below the surface of sickness and problems. The message of badger is to face your adversaries to keep them from having power over you. Stand up for what is right, defend yourself and your belongings. Try to write for self-expression—"

"Surely, Badgers do not write! Isn't this silly? I mean don't any of these animals show cowardice or greed?" the woman in blue asked.

"This is a holistic approach to healing. Each animal suggests a different approach. Badger is an anti-social animal who does not communicate well. Badger may not be direct but his jaws are very strong and symbolically represent the powerful expression of stories, which are the symbolic means of relating to others. Badger is Keeper of Stories."

"Well, what else?" Brigid asked. "I'm having trouble seeing past the cutesy drawings. Maybe you could have cloud cards or day cards: 'Hi. I'm Tuesday; I am a deep blue and sound like a cello; my medicine for you is to relax. My mess—whatever.'"

Some days were like this, Ann thought; why does this woman of some obvious power want to know about western animals? But, she continued and turned the fifth card.

"Crow is a very intelligent, curious bird, who makes a great sentinel. Crow prefers the height of the tallest trees to keep watch. He will work with other crows to steal food rather than hunting for it. Crow is master of movement and illusion. Crow is the fearless guardian of hidden and sacred things. He is a trickster who knows when to reveal his presence and when to stay hidden. When crow enters your life, then it is time for you to interpret signs, omens and dreams. The medicine of Crow is always to be prepared to take advantage of hidden opportunities. The message of Crow is to trust your intuition.

Practice shape shifting. Take a class in Shamanism—"

"Crow offers classes? You all practice shapeshifting here? Can you?"

"No, I only interpret," and Ann turned her head to look for a moment at the lake, not used to being interrupted or teased.

Ann turned the final card, "The medicine of Deer is gentleness and grace. The message of Deer is to be alert and know when—"

"I don't want to hear about deer. Try a different card." Ann thought about the message as she shuffled the cards. Deer knew when to walk away, when to be compassionate and forgiving, when to trust, when to make new friends and try something new. She pulled out Bear. "The Medicine of Bear is strength and dreaming and stamina. The message of Bear is to seek knowledge through meditation, to go inside—"

"No, let's skip the bear, too, yawn."
Ann could not figure this out. Why not learn from the Bear, who represented shamanic journeying in dreams and visions.

"Another?" she asked too politely. The other woman nodded. Ann started speaking before the card was exposed, "Rattlesnake is symbolic of death and rebirth. In ancient times, they were symbols of the Great Mother Goddess—"

"No, no more on this snake!" Brigid recoiled. The serpent was her symbol, the Triple Goddess, but not represented in this awful way.

"Are you in a transitional period?" Ann asked, mistaking distaste for fear. "You know, you could be more powerful if you spent more time outdoors meditating," she said, noting the white pallor of the other's skin. "Would you like to sign up for a Goddess workshop next week?"

Brigid's mouth opened but closed quickly. She tilted her head slightly and fixed the other with her pale eyes, but she did not speak, although the air between them was electric. A card fell on the floor breaking the connection.

Ann spoke hurriedly, without lifting the card, "Otter is a curious, playful, aquatic, carnivorous animal in the weasel family, found in lakes, marshes, streams, and rivers. The medicine of—"

"Yes, I know," Brigid said quietly, "it is the message of

51

the comedian, to enjoy going with the flow—"

"—is feminine energy. Sorry, you were saying? Perhaps you want something else?"

Brigid bent gracefully and picked up the card, "I know this being. Her connection to water links her to Goddess energy. Water is the ancient symbol of female creative force. The message is universal love, not personal, by releasing the negative emotions, like anger, jealousy—I fear I do not always take that to my breast. Otter medicine, hmmm," and she smiled. Then she rose to leave.

On an impulse Ann took the next card and gave it to her.

Brigid took the card and looked at the image of a coyote. The words said that Coyote loved to joke and could be contrary, that his medicine was to strive for a balance between wisdom and folly. Brigid said, as she was looking at it, "Yes, the noble lord of scavenging, the bane of roadkill, the old and the weak. How could there be a challenge from him?"

She handed the card back, waved her hand in acknowledgment, and swept from the room.

Ann looked at the card—Coyote's face had been replaced by a twisted thumbprint. Then, she thought of something and got out her Tarot cards. On the Empress card was the face of the woman who had just left. Ann's knees felt weak, so she sat on the floor.

Brigid had noticed that her golden ring had turned black when she touched the Coyote card. She knew she was in danger and had to flee or to kill this shapeshifter dog, this Coyote. Dogs were held in high regard by her people, the Tuatha de Danan. In fact, they were the archetypal symbol of shapeshifters.

Meanwhile, on the other side of the lake, Wakanda was trying to explain the Irish legends to Coyote. "The Lady of the Lake is older than the Arthurian romances, and older than Celtic Christianity—she is the Irish Goddess Brigid, a primal Dark Mother Goddess and patroness of Shamanism."

"Why should we pay attention to some old has-been?" Coyote drolled. "She sounds like a picture of shoe-leather," Coyote said as he chewed on his right front footpad.

Wakanda looked at that large foot, then continued: "It is hard to picture the Lady of the Lake clearly. In most Arthurian material, she is called Morgan. As Morgan le Fay, she is the seductress who arranges Arthur's downfall, but also, paradoxically, the one who takes him away to Avalon to be healed of his mortal wounds. As 'The Lady of the Lake,' she holds the sword Excalibur out of the waters for Arthur."

"Who's Arthur? Arthur Clarke? Arthur Murray?" Coyote stopped worrying his foot pad and looked at his mate. "So, she's both good and evil? Isn't everyone?" Coyote snorted.

"In Ireland and ancient Britain, there was a trinity of goddesses named Brigid, the Exalted One, a poetess whom poets worshipped. She had two sisters, who had the same name as her, women of healing and of smith-work respectively, who were also goddesses. She herself was a Triple Goddess, simultaneously a virgin, mother and crone; sometimes she had different names, Badb a crone and fury, who could become a wolf or crow, and Dana, the virginal aspect—"

"Yea, I'll bet. I saw her in 'Susi does Sun City'," said Coyote.

"Be quiet, this is not funny!"

"Neither was Dana, wow, more like spunk-inspiring."

"Zip it. The idea of a goddess-trinity shares some characteristics with the three Fates of Greek mythology or the three Norns of Norse mythology."

"I hope she is not related to that oaf, Blokey or Lowkey," Coyote sniffed.

"As goddess of poetry, Brigid is implicitly associated with Celtic shamanism. The Irish made a direct connection between poets and shamans. Song is magic: The word enchant derives from a root word meaning to sing. In early Irish culture the word for poet also meant prophet. In nearly all the shamanic cultures, the shaman in trance receives incantations that are appropriate to sing for various purposes."

"I was, am, a shaman," Coyote reminded her. "I learned to be one. I completed basic training. To be a shaman I suffered through terrible hunger and real cold. I didn't sleep for weeks. I was overwhelmed by the signs of spirits who taught me how to reach them at 3:00 a.m. I learned a special spirit language. I mean, it was hard. I earned the title. I was alone, knowing that wisdom is found in solitude, not the bustle of everyday life. It had to be solitude and suffering," he noticed Wakanda's expression, "Okay, if I have to pay attention, what was she like?" Coyote sighed.

"She lies under a bull hide in a windowless house, waiting to receive the visions that inspired her poetry. And, when she did, she would conduct her worshippers on journeys to another world, through dreams, poetry, ritual, and trance."

"So, she was a slacker working in the dark; sounds like a hacker. We could ask her for a vision. How do we contact her?" he asked.

"Simple, just say 'Sing, goddess, of the bravery of Arthur.' She had shamanic mastery over fire. As fire goddess, she had a perpetual fire kept burning at her temple, Kildara, even after it had become a convent and her vestals became nuns. She had mastery of the fire of the forge, for she is the goddess of the magical art of smithcraft."

"So, she could fix the axle on a Pinto?" Coyote said innocently.

"In those stories, Excalibur, the sword that symbolizes Arthur's kingship, is forged by women in Avalon, which was called The Isle of Apples. Brigid also had a magical apple orchard, and as she was accomplished in smithcraft, she may have even made that sword."

"Computers and swords, wow. I don't like history. Can we go out to eat? Please?" Coyote begged.

"In a minute, this is important. This is about more than human history. This is about myth and power. This can affect us, now. For instance, Brigid is a trickster and shape-shifter. In one old legend, sovereignty was bestowed on Irish kings by a hideous hag who guarded a well; only the rightful king could force himself to embrace and kiss her, whereupon she transformed herself into a beautiful woman and gave him to drink from the well. The king had to ask formally, "Who are you?" And, she replied: 'My name is Sovereignty.' Listen, the sword of Arthur's sovereignty, Excalibur, came to him out of a lake. The Lady of the Lake is a shadow of this goddess Sovereignty. She is hideous and beautiful, evil and good; she is a manipulative enchantress and a giver of good things, in true universal, ambiguous Trickster fashion."

"I don't understand. So, she's a shadow or Sovereignty? A trickster, really? Crow thinks of himself as a trickster, but—"

"Have you forgotten Legba, the African Trickster?"

"Don't mention that name again. It smells of rotten nuts."

"Here is one of her tricks. She asked a bishop for title to the land of her shrine. He refused. She asked only for what could be covered by her cloak, so he swore that she could have that much. But, when she threw her cloak, it spread in glittering billows over hills and vales. The Bishop was enraged at being tricked, but he had sworn and her sacred place was thus preserved."

"Not an original story. Queen Dido did the same to get land for Carthage," Coyote noted.

"Itsayaya, I'm impressed. Where did you learn that?"

"History channel."

"Hmmm. Well, her shrine was the Church of the Oak, which was the World Tree, an indestructible gateway to other worlds, where she could seek knowledge. As a shaman she has to be able to change shape or fly, because these worlds are so distant."

"And, what are these shapes, pray tell?"

"Hawk certainly, or others, I'm not sure."

"Buzzard? Fly?"

Wakanda ignored her mate for a moment, then continued, "Perhaps her cleverest trick was to transform herself from a goddess into a Christian saint, thus having the very Church that opposed Irish paganism perpetuate her name and lore. That is something that we have not been able to do—have a St. Wakanda or St. Coyote," Wakanda concluded, rubbing her paw over her nose.

"Was she like a Horse goddess?"

"You were listening," Wakanda was amazed. "She watches over powerful people from birth to rebirth. In the fire of Her forge, or the water of Her womb, She transforms an initiate; She is the source of vision and wisdom, the giver of spiritual or temporal power. The draught of Her vessel, be it Well or Grail, nourishes, heals, and inspires."

"Grail? So what happened with the Christians?" Coyote asked.

"Druid women had respect, and the Christian church cult could not allow that. They called them witches, evil women who would rebel against Rome, who would conduct Human sacrifices of wicker men. There are underground druid cults now. The women appear with flicks of silver on their faces, giving them a masklike appearance—"

"Masks, okay!"

"Coyote, don't underestimate her, or be fooled by a pretty mask. She is the fearsome, spell-wreaking Morgan and the devouring Ceridwen. She takes the souls of the dead to their after-life or restoration across the sea, beneath Her apple trees. And She speaks to us yet, in dream and myth. We lie still in the dark folds of Her cloak, waiting for the moment when She will turn it over to reveal the fire of the stars."

"You admire her? Sounds like a good match for Loki. Will there be a test?"

"Let's eat. What can you catch?" And, she ran off first.

"Who are you?" asked Wakanda, keeping her eyes directly on her.

Brigid answered: "Just a simple Irish woman."

"When did you come over?" Wakanda asked.

"About 1870."

"And what have you been doing?"

"Just living the simple life."

"Where?"

"In Chicago. My, you are a fount of questions. When did you come over?"

"I was born here, about 30,000 years ago."

"You don't look older than me," Brigid offered, her smile strained; she looked at the woman in front of her wearing a simple brown dress and a necklace with amber.

"I don't believe I can be more than 15,000 years or so older," Wakanda said, and noticed the dark blue cloak that swirled around Brigid's legs. She thought she saw stars flickering behind the cloak, or in the cloak. She felt herself drifting towards the darkness. She lifted her head up with difficulty and said: "Can I offer you an apple?"

"Thanks, that's almost all I eat. At least four a day."

Wakanda smiled, but decided to keep her guard up, by recounting a story while they talked. She wondered if she could fool this woman with invisibility. Maybe later. The two talked about the long migrations of plants, animals and people.

Then Brigid said suddenly, "It is almost new years eve. I have to get ready."

"Is this the first day of winter, after summer's end?"

"Yes, Summer and its harvest symbolize life and Winter and its cold, dark nights symbolize death."

"Yes, of course, have a good celebration," and the two carefully went in opposite directions.

Wakanda wondered what Brigid had planned. She remembered that the boundaries between the worlds of the living and the worlds of the dead became blurred on the night before and the spirits of the dead could roam the earth and create chaos. Some people believed that spirits searched for bodies to possess on this night, now called Halloween, a perfect night for masks. On this night, also, the

Druids could receive prophesies from the spirits roaming the earth, as bonfires were built and living sacrifices were burned. They clothed themselves in costumes made from animal heads and skins, then danced around the bonfire, told fortunes, and waited for the dark night to bring in the new year. The costumes scared off spirits wanting to possess them for the winter and the noisy dance kept spirits far from the living. Wakanda had to keep Coyote from going out tonight.

Later, after being careful not to be followed, she told Coyote of the talk, "Coyote, she is very dangerous. Do not screw around with her. She is strong. She made the transition from pagan to saint, so she knows her way around the modern world better than you."

Coyote smiled. He had heard the words 'screw,' 'her,' 'strong.' And, he doubted she had ever stolen the sun or even a car.

Wakanda recognized that smile and sighed, knowing he was going to get toasted pretty soon. She said, "Listen, seriously, this hag is a shaman, a shapeshifter." As she nuzzled him, she took a bite out of his leg.

"Awww, why? Want to play rough, huh?" And, Coyote jumped her.

And, she knew she could keep him safe for another day.

Coyote could not stand the suspense. He had to see this monster for himself. So, he followed her and stalked her, then let himself be seen. He sat and waited in the field by the edge of the trees and waited to see what she would do. Coyote saw her coming wordlessly towards him. She was beautiful with a form-fitting blue leotard and a short jacket of yellow and blue feathers. Her mouth was open and her eyes were wide; her hair blowing back. She must want him badly. He took a deep breath. He assumed she wanted sex, until he saw her big knife.

Then he remembered Wakanda's warning and immediately took the mask of a bluebird. As he flew up towards the trees, the shadow of a hawk crossed his path, and he knew that she had changed and wanted to eat him, literally. Bad news that. He dove into the pine and flew to the higher smaller branches. Her larger wings prevented her from getting close enough to swallow him, but he was panicking, now.

He dropped to the ground and turned into a rabbit to run. She dropped too, and turned into a coyote. That was a bitch! He was able to twist faster, but he knew she could keep going longer.

He raced out of the root tangle and headed towards Mulberry Creek, ducking under shrubs and widening his gyres of racing.

When he reached the creek, he dove in and took the form of a trout going downstream. He looked back as a long brown body dove in—otter! This was not good. She must have hunted like this before.

He flicked under a bank, then under a stone where he changed into a dragonfly, He stayed there for a time. The otter was not in sight. Must be far downstream, he thought. He waited forever, 26 minutes, just in case. Then, he flew up towards a low branch. But, a tongue wrapped around him and he entered the maw of a frog. 'Wrong arc angle' was Coyote's last thought.

She waited until he was really digested. She did not want to end up giving birth to him, like she did to that troublesome Welsh bard, Taliesin. She had a few more light meals of flies while waiting for the dragonfly wings to be excreted. Now, she was finished with him and could eliminate that troublesome old hag Wakanda.

This was odd, observed Brigid. Wakanda had disappeared. In fact, not even a crow was to be found. She was getting tired of this constant searching. Maybe the hag dog had gone back to Wyoming or whatever backward state she had come from. She needed to restore her strength and she knew just where. She traveled quickly to a secret place. She stood before her tree, a holly, which was the tree of protection, prophecy, and magic.

She spoke the sacred words at the entrance to the circle: "I am Brid, beloved of Erin, spirit of fire, healer of ills, protector of life, woman of power, mother of all. I create, inspire, and make magic. I am young and virginal, a vital mother, old and eternal. I am power personified. I am a wolf, a wren—"

She noticed that the oak tree on the other side of the altar seemed to have a dark spot. As she walked by the altar, a blackberry vine with thorns caught her dress. A chalice of blackberries spilled. She skirted the old water well, in case something was not right. Oh, dear, the oak tree had started to rot.

As she leaned over, and touched the darker wood, the sky pushed her in. She tried turning, but could not. She tried using the tree, but could not contact it or influence it. She was trapped in its hollow. "Ohh! AAhhhh!" she screamed. Who had done this? Merlin? Was he back? Something fell on her head. She looked up. She could see half of a hazelnut lodged in her hair above her eye.

Another half hit her cheek.

"For inspiration," the words fell down the hollow trunk, "for the next 500 years."

"Who are you? Why would—"

"You know who I am."

"Yes, yes, you. I killed him, you know. It was easier than I thought."

Yes, but he's been dead before. Not a big deal for me."

"Yes, but you will never find him. His remains are out to sea by now. When I get—achoo!" Her nose had been tickled by a few dog hairs floating down. She groaned, knowing what that meant. "I will find you later, and I will not be so kind." She fumed. Of all trees to be trapped in—the oak, a tree of magic for men.

"Goodbye, I hope your tree does not get made into a toilet seat!" Wakanda said, smiling and putting the rest of Coyote's leg hairs into her medicine kit. Now, if she could just find Fox in a reasonable time. She ate some blackberries while she walked.

Brigid let out a loud, long wail to show her unhappiness. She was the queen of keen, as it were. She tried to invoke Uath MacImoman, the horror born of terror, the shapeshifter who could take any form. She would implore him to rise to this challenge. She remembered that she had on her the means of escape from the female Coyote: Poison, a water element; fire; stick, the earth element; and rope, the air element. Maybe only the air element would work here. She would try it after a good rest.

She quieted and thought: The circle was still open, but the vine moon would soon set. Perhaps she could outsmart the trap. She let go of everything and relaxed. She sank deeper into herself, letting go of the connections to the moon and tree, of the physical world. The burdens fell away like loose clothes.

"Fox, be a dear and jump over this purse, would you?"

"Is that all I am? Just a reboot function for the Coyote computer?" Fox answered absently, as he planned a surprise for the people of Happy Hollow Woodbine west of Kansas City.

'Coyote computer, hmmm,' thought Wakanda. "Yes, of course," she said absently. She put a few of the hairs on the ground and Fox jumped over them.

Suddenly, Coyote exploded from the hairs, spitting in disgust and checking to see if he still had four legs. He looked at Fox and nodded, then saw Wakanda and said, "Oopppsss, you're right—she's good. I'm starving! Anything to eat? No? I'll just go see what I can get," and Coyote ran off.

Wakanda looked at Fox, who shrugged.

Coyote was very hungry and wanted to eat the first thing he saw. He saw Spider between two trees. "I need to eat you."

"Wait, why am I in this tree, you ask," said Spider. "I'll tell you. This tree is chief tree of the world. I close my eyes and I can see everything. Wouldn't you like to see?"

"Yes," Coyote admitted.

"Well. Close your eyes and hold on tight." Coyote hugged the tree, but Spider bound him with silk.

Coyote broke loose and said, "The purpose of my life is to eat you."

"The purpose of life is to sleep."

"Not to dream?" Coyote decided to ask advice from Spider, to see if he could find ways to make his life easier.

"Dream? No, I never dream, never have to, that's what my waking life is. You know, you could sleep more if you hunted like I do." Spider was testing the tension on his strands in the web between two branches.

"Yea?" asked Coyote.

"Yea, watch. See when the web vibrates I rush over and bite whoever is waking me up. Then I hav'em for lunch."

"Here, let me try," suggested Coyote, who started to move into the web.

"No!! You're too heavy! You broke a few strands there. Wait a minute—can you spin your own?"

"I don't think so. It comes out

in lumps."

"Well, try to narrow the hole, so it makes a thread."

Coyote narrowed and grunted and something did come out thinner but it had no tensile strength, and it smelled.

"No, never do. That won't trap anyone, I mean, unless they step in it; although it does look sticky enough. No, I think you need something more like a rope. Can you get rope?"

"Listen, eight-eyes, I can get a rope, but I don't see how that will hold a deer."

Coyote had to go to town to Ace to get a good hemp rope. While he was shopping, he bought some string, superglue, library paste, and flypaper. Then the newspaper, coffee and a donut. When he came back, he started eating and drinking as he sketched out his idea for a perfect web.

Spider reminded him not to tie knots in it, just make sure that it crossed often at certain angles. Coyote hung one length of rope between two trees, then he put glue all over it and hung another length at an angle. When he tested it the glue was dry, and did not hold anything, so he put the paste on it.

Spider was busy making a model web for Coyote to follow, all the while shouting instructions. On his own, Coyote put flypaper down on the ground under the giant web.

A deer came by to see what was going on. When Coyote tried to shoo her into the web, his feet stuck to the flypaper; when he grabbed the rope to steady himself, his paws were stuck. When he struggled, the ropes fell from the trees and covered him.

Spider told Coyote a story, all the while calculating if he and his hundred kids could eat Coyote from the outside. "Once people came to me, afraid of crazy Loon. One asked, 'What shall we do? We must go to the south, we must run away.'

Another one said 'No, Loon will catch us if we go south. Let us go to the north.'

A third said 'No, let us go to the east.'

'Let us go to the west,' said Coyote, that would be you, remember. 'No, she will catch us there.'

'Where shall we go?'

'We must go up to the sky.'

'How shall we go up? We must hurry before Loon gets up.'

'Who will take us up to the sky?' said Eagle, 'I can only carry one of you. Maybe Spider can lift you with his rope. Ask him.'

'They did, I was the man. The people had a great sack and they all got into it. 'Hurry up,' I said. Then I made the rope come down from the sky and tied it to the sack. 'Who is going in first?' I asked.

Coyote said, 'My friend, I will be the first.'

'All right, but be careful,' I said.

"Wait a minute! I'm Coyote. I don't remember that."

"Do you remember what you did last Market Day?"

"No."

"Then how can you remember every little adventure? Anyway, he, you, got in, and all the rest got in after him. I said 'Stretch!' to the sack and it did so, stretched to the north, south, east, and west, till all the people got in. Then I pulled the rope and pulled the sack up. My finest hour."

Spider looked at the flypapers on Coyote's feet and noticed 5 flies had been caught already. Maybe he would not have to eat Coyote after all.

Coyote said: "Seriously, you told me I could see everything from the tree. How come I can't? I want to see everything."

"I was lying to trap you. If you really want to see everything, throw your eyes to the top of the tree."

"You do it first," Coyote demanded.

"I don't need to. What do you want to see?"

"I need to know if Buffalo is coming."

"Just assume he is and untangle those ropes. You're scaring away the flies, now."

Coyote untangled himself and walked away disappointed. He had an important contest to go to, or he would have eaten that arrogant eight-legged freak.

Turtle was rapping at the Candy Rapper night club:
  "Gotta bong near my dong
    It's a song its so long
    Hey, get back, its not wrong
    Just got to show you how now
    It is—"

Wakanda said, "I don't think rapping is the way."
          "What? I am a megarapper," argued Coyote.
      "People want to hear soothing sounds. They don't want to be
reminded of violence and inequity."
                              "People or animals?"
      "Animals are people; they just wear masks."
                              "What? What do you mean?"
Wakanda took off her face and a human face was there,
"A nice face,' Coyote thought, 'reminded him of someone,
an actress or someone really famous.'

          Then she made the human face disappear and there was a blur
above her shoulders. 'How does she do that?' Coyote thought.
He pulled on his nose, but nothing came off; then he sneezed and
something came out.

                  An invisible tongue licked his chest, a voice
saying, "You're as bad as the pups."
                          "But, how? Why can't—
      "Listen, and watch. All souls wear masks to fit in their places.
You can take them off and be bare. You can make them
out of your breath—"

                  "Is that what you do?" Coyote asked.
      Wakanda raised her paw and her face reappeared.
                      "Breath?" Coyote asked, then huffed.
      Wakanda said, "It's okay, I can give you some pointers, but let's
focus on your howling, first."

Coyote tired quickly and looked over the audience; they seemed to be
older than normal rap aficionados. Coyote had an inspiration.
He would go country, maybe Conway Twitty or Mickey Newbury.
He had to wait for Turtle to finish, and then was the interminable
Prairie Dog trying to bark out some rhymes on 'earth-moving' or
something.

Finally it was his turn and he took the mike:
    "The old 43 train whistle didn't wake me
    But the wind from the train rustled my papers
    And I wished there was more pages in the news
    So the rain wouldn't soak me down to my shoes
    Oh, please, give me a break, don' let them take
    The memories of you cause that's all I do
    Is see you in the past and if I don't last
    The rum won't preserve my—"
Coyote's voice was cracking, and the tear in his eye
just wouldn't drop. A pause for effect—

Then Crow glided down and took the microphone
and beat out the terminal blues:
    "Comin out aint goin out, if there no way back
    goin in may be comin in, if the lines are tracks
    guess better be gone now thumbin out o town
    disappearin down a smokin hole see me goin down
    some words just wont do baby, not a two-way street
    some words make a fire, some words fan the heat
    but less you got more to cool em, ice em stop em,
    aint no words get you out, oh no, none, uhh, ummm.
    i got a case of the terminal blues, long-term, life-time blues
    didn't even lie, jus sentenced for some crime
    nothin bout a trial just sentenced given life
    wish this prison had some walls, a place to go
    and if i ever got there, baby, id just know
    i got a case of the terminal blues
    miserable cold, never too old, terminal blues
    illinois central out of track, no soft bed for this poor black.
    bus station bus end of the line, no more money no way back;
    got to walk on to get past too tired too late to get on, too dark,
    don't know where i am, can't read signs, got to lie down,
    don't care, cover me with paper something say i can't last
    oh, long-term life-time terminal blues
    wish i had warmer shoes, more pages in the news—ruhhh!"

The crowd applauded him not Coyote, who raced for the mic,
but Crow tossed it to Fox, who had his own drum to beat:
    "Call this the suicidal in-line blues; goes like this:
    Ain't no pride in working the lines

no need for stuff we bolt together
but the money is enough to make
the next payments on the stuff
we bought to live better—heh
So, you just sit, my simple pretty
plan for kids for meaning in our life
without thinking where they get
the meaning in their own—heh.
No matter what I say, these words
can't explain, make up the loss you feel
so contented in your private world
never know I could kill—heh!
But the ever-moving line keep producing
there is no freedom that direction
but there's freedom out this door
waits the other side somewhere
won't have this burden any more."

Coyote tried to pounce on the magic black stick so he could finish his
dirge to rain on trains, but a young girl caught it and started:
"Can we resume our innocence?
Where was I before I learned things I wished to learn no more?
Has my body not renewed itself My soul forgotten the pain?
Must I be burdened by experience Or can I start forgetting?
Are we such incorrigible gold That we just tarnish with time
Awaiting polish to shine again? Or are we transmuted by constant
Additions of experience towards A critical mass and change?
Can we—"

Finally Coyote got the microphone in his mouth—
          Hey, that girl's breath smelled familiar—
He pulled it out and started wailing, "Wooo woooo
     That train is going, going down the line
     and it's leaving me blowing, blowing—"
"—out my ass, just some gas, out my ass," some young man was
singing over Coyote.
                    The audience was raucous, Coyote was raucous,
everyone was, but, it made little difference, the crowd was chanting
its decision, "Crow, Crow!"
                    And so Crow became the new Desert Idol.

"Coyote? Have you forgotten dinner tonight?" Wakanda mentioned.

Coyote never forgot food, but this was a social commitment. Although Otter had invited them to dinner, he didn't want fish. But, they went and were not more than 89 breaths late.

"Welcome to my holt. This is my bitch Musella. We're going to eat outside in the back under the tree."

Musella hung back shyly, smaller than Otter with a slender face and body, two tone brown over white with a black-tipped tail longer than her entire body.

Wakanda gave the other woman a mouse wrapped in a mushroom. Mrs. Deer whispered to her mate, "She's a weasel!"

"Otter! Lonnie you water-dog," Coyote greeted his friend warmly, hugging him closely and whispering in his ear, "who's the weasel?"

Otter bit the tender pad on Coyote's paw, "Don't. She has a really nice, long tail. I wouldn't—Owww!"

Otter had nipped the end of Coyote's nose. "—wouldn't want to step on it by accident I was going—" Otter had turned and was greeting Wakanda, who had brought him a small shellfish wrapped in a mushroom.

Wakanda bussed Musella's face so their whiskers brushed, "My what a beautiful coat you have."

"And, yours, I would die for those subtle colors."

Deer was ruminating to Dear about why they were invited. Usually, he was the main course. But, this was a nice change.

Otter announced: "We have a frog and crayfish appetizer for you. And fish for dinner, with a side dish of snake—Musella caught it this morning. I did make a lettuce and grass salad for the Deer. For dessert, quail eggs, with dandelion heads, buds and acorns for the Deer."

They were talking about interesting experiences from their pasts. Musella had been an exchange student in Australia, a continent with many rodents, kangaroos and bats, but no weasels. Deara had been chosen Miss October for a Calendar of Wildlife. Otter had been working on double somersaults into the creek. Everyone seemed very happy. Coyote took out his new mobile phone to call the Pups, since Uncle Lasagna, his last choice, was baby-sitting.

"Hey, is that one of those new, MePhones, with the Swiss army knife in it?" Deer asked.

"Yea, it's totally cool. Has like a thingy that prints pictures, too."

The males were pointing to buttons. Coyote wanted to try a prank call on Eagle, but Deer refused to scream in fake pain.

The females were talking about their young. Musella had not mated yet, but she was hoping for a large romp of her own. Everyone was enjoying his or her food.

"Is everyone finished?" Musella asked.

The Deer were still chewing, but Coyote volunteered, "They'll be rechewing for days. Let's get to dessert."

As they were eating the eggs, Coyote asked Deer, "How come I never see you two together?"

"Oh, I just hang around with the bucks. The fawns don't need me to show 'em how to cross the road."

"Do they cross by themselves?" Wakanda asked.

Dear said, "Yes, I taught them to look both ways. It's been a week without a fatality. Those humans just go too fast. I wish—" and her black nose twitched with emotion.

Walking home in the late evening, Wakanda, said, "That went well. Thank you for not eating Deer— I heard Deer offer you a bite, but it would have been bad manners—and thank you for not offering Otter a bite out of me. And, thank you for not inviting Eagle or Vulture to Otter's party. How was your fish?"

"Fresh, and thank you for not going all invisible or showing the women how to make masks. And, thanks for not noticing me drop a crayfish on the dirt."

"I noticed that; also, you gave your snake to Otter and took his frog."

"Revenge, a little," Coyote said cryptically.

Their hips and tails touched as they walked.

Coyote was walking down the alley, when he heard approaching thunder. He knew this was where the new gods had chosen their palaces.

"Are you the thunder god?" Coyote asked timidly.
"No, man, biker. Listen to this! VROOOM!!" and Karl rode off with a squeal of tires.

Coyote saw a big cat, maybe a wild cat, pacing beside a dumpster.
"Hey, what god are you?" Coyote asked jokingly.
"I am Hank-Ra," the cat replied seriously.
"Hank-Ra? What kind of name is that. Two first names or two last names?"
"Had to be joined equally, see, I'm part cowboy, part Egyptian deity. My sister, Mer-seti II, is cool too."
"Mer?" Coyote was getting tired of the habit of young people to contract every word to one syllable; it made for a short and mysterious language.
"Short for Mercedes."
"I am here," Coyote began sonorously, "to be part of the new pantheon, perhaps to head it."
Hank-Ra was used to stuffed egos and replied simply, "Why don't we meet the whole team." And they went inside a nondescript door. But, inside, it looked like a Mayan temple, with plaster masks on the walls. Hank-Ra stopped before the first group he saw.
"Coyote, this is Palimetheus, brother of Prometheus."
"Hey, I took fire back from mankind; gave it back to the trees."
"And Hypometheus," who just nodded, shyly.
"Who is that woman over there?" Coyote asked.
"That's Auntie Metheus."
"Just huddle for warmth dears," she said.
"And, this is COmetheus." Hank-Ra said.
"No need to huddle, soon every place will be warm," he said.

Coyote was tired already, "Just how many gods are there?!"
"You know," said Hank-Ra, "I have been thinking about this for a while. We are the fourth, I mean fifth, wave of gods."
"You mean there might be a sixth? More gods?"
"As long as things change, everything changes, even gods. Think

about it. The first wave was animal spirits. Then the second wave produced gods like Zeus, an air god; Poseidon, water; Hades underground; Pan nature; Aphrodite love and beauty; Hermes god of trade and fortune—"

"Yea!" said Coyote, pumping his fist, "love ya, Herm!" Coyote was always excited to hear about his friend, another irresponsible, lusty male.

"—then Hera marriage and family; Nemesis divine anger to humans; Hephaestus craftsmanship metalworking; and Ares war. These were the kind of gods that people had in small communities.

"But, when they moved to cities, and had to mix with other people who had other gods, the cities developed more universal gods, such as Yahweh, Buddha, and Zoroaster. These were the third wave, sophisticated urban gods that many groups could agree to worship, big enough to be inclusive, but nebulous enough for people to see what they wanted in them.

"The fourth wave you already met I hear, the new gods of machine images and progress. Humanity, who worships herself; Media god of reduced information and displayer of partial data; Growth, Hater of Limits Lover of Infinite; Progress, Inflation, the 3-headed Profit—each head larger that the one before; Personalprofit, Shortermprofit, and Megaprofit; Bottomline; War, served by a few demigods like Shockenawe and Police-action; Clock, the master god of machines; Sports, Fashion, Celebrity, Sales, Falsedream, Loserworker, Collaterdamage, Welfare, Art, Artdirector, Advertising, Payback—the goddess of vengeance, Humiliation, Death, Disease, Plague, Nature, Wildlife, Weather, Earthquake, Comet, and so on. So different, yet so the same. These gods have already started to fail and are becoming impotent. People will desert them soon.

"Leaving things open to the fifth wave—starting with me. You might think I am a hybrid of new and old, and I suppose I am. Hank-Ra. Hank-Ra."

"You like saying your name," observed Coyote. "You say it!" ordered Hank-Ra.

"Maybe later. So, who are your pals in the new surf, I mean turf?"

"Some are from the breakup and downsizing of Media; they are Texter, Gamer, and Gambler. Sustainability is growing in importance. Some may always be big, Sports and Entertainment. A few others such as Growth and Clock are still big, but they depend on Oil—he's big, real big, but he's not as slick as he was. There's Megawealth, the concentrated symbol, and Gigadoodle, of virtual information fame and her spouse Metadata. Doom is big, now—"

"Oh, I played that!"

"No, this is like one of the four horsemen or something. Collapse, I can't keep track. Kitsch, Glitch and Ploof.

"Poof? Law Firm?" Coyote asked.

"No, Poof! is the god of cliches and templates for writing. Ploof is the godlet of mild mistakes. One the Demon Lites."

"Well, can I meet them?" Coyote asked.

"Sure, come with me."

They went past another entry way to a deep interior room that looked like it might have had dried blood on the walls.

There they were met by Texter at the door. He let in Hank-Ra and his guest, although he lifted his eyes from his ipod and lifted his nose at Coyote.

Coyote looked at the niches in the walls, each filled with a head of an older god or demi-god. It reminded him of the den of a hunter where the walls would display the heads of the prey. It reminded him of the older tradition of putting the heads of your enemy on pikes. And still older, women putting the heads of animals on poles. Everything was heads up.

Coyote was wearing his old Geraldo Riviera mask, and posing as a religious 'good news' man, but everybody seemed to recognize him.

The gods were participating in a team-building exercise, "Catch the Snap." More like a team irritating exercise, Coyote thought, looking foolish makes us all equal. Sports was leading it. When they looked his way, Coyote shook his head, knowing that he would snap for real and be forced to eat one of them. Coyote saw Humanity right away, sprawling over three chairs. Humanity had taken over as head god, after Media had been broken up.

"I see the fat lady is finally head of the circus," Coyote mumbled.

Humanity still had it in for Coyote. He was irritating too many suburbanites by crapping on their lawns and eating the smaller cats and dogs. He was simply urinating on too many posts and signs. She could not be appeased, and Coyote would not give her any peas if he had any. She turned away and whispered something to her cohort,

70

Biggy Big, while casting a baleful eye on Coyote as he moved around the room.

Coyote was thinking about these mean, powerful, rich, new gods. The new Fruits of the Earth, as Andre Gide might have said, the new gods of desire, sensation and instinct, with their goals of adventure and excess. Or maybe, as J.K. Toole thought, the gods of Chaos, Lunacy and Bad Taste had gained ascendancy. Coyote wondered where Success, Excess and Sexcess, the ESS brothers, came into it. Who was Couchpotato, anyway?

Coyote waved to Weather, who waved warmly at him, but then she was doing everything warmly now. Artdirector turned his back and sniffed.

Coyote pulled on his long moustache and looked at Clock, who was explaining something to Oil about the sun and plants, and being past his peak.

Oil replied loudly, "I am *at* my peak and I should have a century or more of Power. Don't count me out, just because you can go solar. You need me to make the big shit, the iron and engines."

Sports looked up at the word 'iron' but decided it was not the same and went back to pointing to people to snap.

Gambler came up to Coyote and offered, "Give you 5 to 1 that Oil doesn't last over 20 years." Coyote looked at him and pulled out a dollar bill. Gambler said, "No. Nothing under a million, sorry." Sustainability shook his head sadly.

Coyote decided to have a secret meeting with the god Gamer.
"I am Coyote. Can we talk somewhere?"
"Sure, we can use the floating security room," said Gamer, a lanky guy wearing a cowboy hat and a black eye patch. They walked up to a transparent glass room and frosted the glass with a switch.

"What is your game?" Gamer asked.
"Mostly I chase and eat it, but I play a lot too," Coyote answered.
Gamer wanted Coyote to be in a new Game, "You would be perfect, sneaky, clever … I can help you make an avatar to represent you. How do you see yourself?"

"Tall, deep-chested, narrow-hipped, long-legged, strong-profile, very smart—I'm hungry."
"Short-attention span, hypersexual needs—"
"Don't forget the wavy hair," Coyote said.

Gamer said, "Hey, I'm worth $40 billion a year annual revenue, globally. I didn't get this rich by forgetting anything. Check out my blogs!"

"What is a glog?" Coyote asked, "Excrement? Is that it?"

"Sort of like brain shit, full of undigested stuff, useful for dung beetles and termites. Used to be books were the fertile resource."

"Sounds good," Coyote admitted.

"Actually, it's just whatever you are doing now, like eating candy or playing with your—"

"But, why would people be interested in that?"

"Got me, but it works."

"What's this one?"

"The World of Warcrafters. You'll love it. It's like what I do for the government and military."

Coyote watched Gamer point and click up a storm of windows and things. He realized these edutainment games were interactive, nonlinear, user-created masterpieces of interfacing. Fox had told him to talk to the control nerd and Coyote was sure Gamer was it.

Hours later, he met Hank-Ra on the way out.

"Well, what did you learn?" Hank-Ra asked.

"What games teach us. That brute force wins! What skills do they teach us? To set a dial to maximum destructive power before pulling the trigger hundreds of times! Why be subtle. If something irritates you, overwhelm it with shock and awe."

"Wow, you're more subtle than I thought."

"I couldn't get the trigger to go over 10,000 rounds," Coyote confessed, "About the new gods, it could have gone better."

"Perhaps, you shouldn't refer to them as 'The Supremes' all the time," Hank-Ra noted.

Coyote started playing on an old laptop. Gamer had shown Coyote how to navigate around the web. He was searching for sex when he saw a virtual page site. Hmm. He could enter the virtual world, get back to Gamer and create an avatar Coyote that would water the web so to speak. He accidently attached to a virtual printer that could print blueprints into concrete. Coyote thought, 'if concrete why not piss? Real piss?'

When Glenda came in the next morning to her job at Asymmetricalz, she saw the yellow puddle on the floor. Someone had been messing with the printer again.

Interface: Coyote gets Spammed

Coyote turned on his computer and linked in. He was hoping the new gods had sent an invitation to him to rule them. Finally, he got to his email, and excitedly read the emails addressed just for him, all to him at tricknose@dismyth.it He bought the first three things in order.

> From: kipgaugeablewhitley@authorama.com
> Subject: You Can Enlarge Your Penis By 3"
>
> ─────────
>
> From: scrubbiests631@hh-llp.com
> Subject: Viagra 100mg x 60 pills US $ 129.95 buy now
>
> ─────────
>
> From: bpowell@cwbgroup.com
> Subject: Chopard & Hermes Watches $24.99
>
> ─────────

Coyote was still anxious about his penis. He had heard a commercial for a new drug called Extender. One pill to become larger. He meant to try that, too. Maybe if he took 70 at once? Then he decided to scroll down, past the new banner showing a race car domain names.

> From: jewelcowbellboogie@makeupminute.com
> Subject: Last Longer in Bed
>
> ─────────
>
> From: tennisqueen5@performance-additives.com
> Subject: Vagrea, Celias (qqv)
>
> ─────────
>
> From: mimisheater@girlscouts.org
> Subject: Rolex is not for all. Is it for you ?
>
> ─────────

Coyote noticed a pattern after a while: Apparently everyone wanted a larger penis, medicine to keep it erect, and a watch to time it! And a guarantee as well. But, there was more. No, those were popups shilling shampoo.

> From: outriders747@brainsofeurope.com
> Subject: Price for Viagra 100mg x 90 pills $159.95
>
> ─────────
>
> From: kipwhatregilliam@europa.eu
> Subject: Jaeger-LeCoultre replica watch -- Luxury isn't a sin
>
> ─────────

From: amerimoondogs@americancentury.com
Subject: Which Ones Really Work? Top Penis Enlargement Products!

_____

From: vickiballcuevas@hivtest.org
Subject: Lose 20 pounds in 3 weeks

_____

From: carolinareciprocityconn@stylishfetish.com
Subject: Gain 3+ Inches In Length.

_____

From: theronkolkhozcherry@americancatholic.org
Subject: Compare Top 5 Penis Enlargers

_____

From: gene.whitman@marschalekbo.com
Subject: Lose 30 pounds in 2 weeks

_____

From: douglasjeffreycook@bjsbrewhouse.com
Subject: Increase Your Penis Width (Girth) By up to 20%.

_____

From: randallsurtaxstevens@catholicpriests.com
Subject: Increase Your Penis Width (Girth) By up to 30%.

_____

From: underbridge@balston-purina.com
Subject: My take on your response too my blog
I ain't happy about your recent comment on my comment about ...

Oh, no, attack blogs, fast, furious and nonstop. Must be free trolls. Coyote had to quit Firefox and sign back on. He had seen one ad for online degrees; must be for the men sending their blood south of the belt. Somehow everything on the web fit together so nicely to address all of your needs.

From: maribelstaminalanders@time-blog.com
Subject: is ROLEX under 199 w Slap-up accessories?

_____

From: ejectlargespunk@activeware.com
Do you masturbate enough? Here's how to tell!

_____

From: kristinmarialam@xulplanet.com
Subject: Produce Stronger, Rock Hard Erections From badboner to huge meat?
        From bad groaner to good moaner? YES!

_____

From: angelitafaultyisaac@michaelbrecker.com
Subject: Help Stop Premature Ejaculation!

_____

From: yordanka.davidson@kahlenberg.at
Subject: Lose 50 pounds in 2 weeks (ejaculate more)

_____

From: dylanextramaritalmelton@startingpointnh.org
Subject: You Can Enlarge By 5"/Compare Top 5 Penis Enlargers

—————

From: laneflexiblesolis@harvardbusiness.org
Subject: You Can Enlarge Your Penis By 7"

—————

It went on forever, so he gave up reading. The screen was closing
in with popups, slide-bys, and larger banners. Time to quit anyway.
Amazing that they all were writing to him, trying to help him. Maybe
he should order something from everyone.

Then, it occurred to him that there were some strange
players—like what were the Girl Scouts up to, pushing watches? And,
it looked like the Catholic Church was getting proactive about things
relating to sex and procreation!

Coyote was thinking of investing his massive horde of mongongo nuts and his trove of technical things, like the exoskeleton, in the Stock Market, which had lost 50% of its value, and might offer some good bargains for a keen-eyed investor. He went to see Vulture, in the fourth willow by Plum Creek, about wise investing. Vulture was promoting his new capitalistic investment scheme, Vulture Funds. It was simple: 'Gang up the flock, take over some financial carcass and pick it apart, then sell the bones.'

Even though vulture was quite black, when he finally got a mask to wear for human negotiations, it was that of an elderly white banker. "It's easy to rationalize this," Vulture explained, "This is how business is done between rational entities. If something is weak and dying, recycle the meat. We are not 'taking advantage' of the weak.

We are making places for new young strong future weaklings! We are not creating victims, we are opening spaces for others to try— what could be more democratic? That makes the remaining entities more wary and conservative. Once we take over we simply reduce the number of people, the headcount, then reduce their salaries, the dollar count, then make them work faster, the minute count, but finally send much of the work to cheaper people, the bottom-line count. That way everyone gets sorted out in an evolutionary way. Survival of the cheapest as it were."

"But, what about you and the other Directors. You make $600 million each! Each!!" Coyote emphasized.

"And, that's quite cheap, in the scheme of Directors, considering what we do. Why—"

"Is this the seed and grain exchange?" interrupted Rabbit, coming over and standing next to Coyote.

"I call it the 'mouse exchange,'" quipped Coyote.

"No," answered Vulture, "It is the capitol of capitalism, where we inflate value and assign profits."

"Vulture, that is a bubble. It is going to break," Rabbit predicted.

"Nonsense, it may realign with our values, but it cannot break."

"Ridiculous."

"No, really, listen—"

"No, you listen," said Rabbit rabidly. "It is a bubble, and it relies on the suspension of belief and an expectation of large profits, even though it is not the same as a Ponzi scheme. A bubble involves ever-rising, unsustainable prices in an open market—whether shares of stock, housing prices, the price of tulip bulbs, or anything else. As long as buyers are willing to pay ever-increasing prices, sellers can get out with a profit. Bubbles arise naturally out of human greed and foolishness."

Prairie dog had been attracted by the loud voices and came over next to Rabbit. She asked, "But, what about normal people, who get trapped by the cycle?"

Rabbit answered: "They could move elsewhere or rent, but they think it will go up, after they buy, so they get sucked in."

Vulture answered at the same time, "That is why all the participants in my NuPonZ Foundation for Wild Philanimalopy, which gives up to 10% of profits to the Red, Yellow and Green Crosses, are guaranteed through a matching gift program."

"Can I participate?" asked Prairie dog.

"Wait, I want you to get a high-yield investment program called the 'Short-Term Animatarian Financing Transaction' (SHAFT). The proceeds from your investments will be used to finance animaltarian projects around the globe, such as low-cost housing for the poor in developing nations. Of course, this program is licensed by the Federal Reserve and the program has a strong relationship with the International Monetary Fund and the United States Treasury."

"Woa, sign me up, I want to make money," enthused Prairie dog.

"But, that's not all, early investors can expect profits of up to 4,000 percent."

"And, what percentage of that goes to pay commissions to salespeople, to make payments to investors to keep the scheme going, and to pay your own personal expenses?" asked Rabbit.

"I don't want to have to sue you for slander," Vulture said.

Rabbit continued: "Prairie Dog, listen to me. Anyone of any intelligence is vulnerable to deception by an experienced con artist. Everyone has some weakness, and a good con man has the confidence tricks to exploit virtues, like honesty, compassion, or good faith, as well as weaknesses like greed, vanity, or hatred."

"But, I don't have those things. I'm just a simple digger, with a few seeds to grow."

Vulture continued to justify his view: "The universe is becoming more complex. Animals are getting smarter, plants more clever. The same thing is happening with our money, that is, our symbols. Houses become more valuable, really, seriously, land becomes more valuable, but so do inventions and ideas—"

"And speculation and greed?"

"Sadly, no, this is the avian condition, like the human condition, always wanting more, but that doesn't mean that things are worse or flatter."

Although Prairie dog was emptying his cheeks of seeds and grains to invest, Rabbit was not convinced. "This kind of business is not sustainable. The predatory financial regime is like a protection racket that requires boot-licking and rolling over. Corporate democracy subverts the powers of congress and the powers of courts. The goal is to maintain power for as long as possible to profit as much as possible from the helpless prey."

Coyote was thinking about going with the Vulture fund, now, convinced by the idea of helpless prey.

"That is the difference between Vulture culture and Rabbit culture," said Vulture. "We try to grow a profit to lift you out of the daily scramble for water and roots, ha."

"No, your fund, hell civilization, is just a pyramid scheme offered by a pool of deranged confidence men. I'll just save my shoots."

"Did you hear what Owl is trying to do?" asked P-dog, a moment later.

"What trickles down is the spray from the up-flow to the rich!" said Rabbit. "It's the lemons problem all over again. Give the worst land to the natives, give the worst jobs to the Irish, and then give the worst assets—houses, land, banks—to the government to hold. Some of the rich are criminals who break laws to enrich themselves, resulting in fraud and the collapse of the system. Let's execute them," urged Rabbit. "What do you think, Coyote?"

"Sell the whole country to the Swedes. Go on the dole."

Coyote is Rich!

Coyote had lost $10,000 in the Vulture Fund, actually $200,000 in potential profits. He was hanging his head over dinner.
Wakanda said: "You should be grateful for the wealth you have."
"What wealth? I'm not rich, now."
"Remember when you cut down your forest for profit?" Wakanda asked.
"Yes?" Coyote responded, remembering that disappointing disaster, another loss from following the advice of others.
"Well, I replanted it and just left it to grow."
"For me? Can I cut it again, to get money?"
"Well, after I replanted it, I set it up as a trust."
"So, how much is it worth?"
"The land is worth a couple hundred thousand—
"What are we waiting for? I need money for, ah, er, for my campaign against poverty."
"—But the trees are worth $24 million."
Coyote blew out a chunk of mouse. His eyes bulged; both nostrils sucked air big time. He started planning, "You know, with that much—"
"It's a trust."
"So?"
"Only small numbers of trees can be cut, and just to pay taxes. It is certified as a sustainable wild forest."
"But, I could get paid for the work, right?"
"Yes, but never more than $12,000 a year, at $12 an hour," she added, so he would not think he could get $800 an hour.
"Couldn't we disband the Trust?"
"Yes, but only to another trust or nonprofit with similar rules."
"What if a hurricane blew down the trees? I know someone—"
"Natural processes are allowed to operate. We would have to leave them down."
"But, we are part of nature and taking from nature is natural, so we could benefit—"
"But, we cannot take them off the land. Trees need to go back into the soil to keep the system healthy."
"But, what if—" and suddenly Coyote was out of what-ifs. "You mean, I'm rich, but I can't touch it?"

"We are rich—you gave it to me, remember. I am sharing it with you."

"Why did you tell me?" Coyote moaned.

"So you would be happy, like me."

"Oh, joy," said Coyote, thinking 'something else I can't get.'

He had to get rich for real, with real useful disposable assets. He had been rich before, trading stocks in New York, running the Chevrolet Foundation, but then he had left that to pursue other dreams.
The college had been successful, although he had been pressured out by Kankersoar and Glurtus—he had heard that it collapsed. That had been high-maintenance work, also. He took inventory of his successes. A Wall-street mogul, an artist of course, filmmaker, singer/rapper, doctor, rancher, driver, inventor, defective, er detective, and lawyer. Of course he had had failures. He had never been elected. He sometimes chose the wrong kind of mate. Some of his kids had died—well, all of them. The Shaman thing had not played out well; he could not heal or restore anyone. He was being modest, of course, he as knew a shaman was not supposed to always do parlor tricks or show off.

What had he learned? How to buy clothes ... something else. Maybe he should play to his strengths. What were they? Greed, lust, perseverance, adaptability—He was perfect for politics. Why was he not popular? It shouldn't be a popularity contest. He should be chosen by somebody because of his superior skills and great vision. Maybe he could buy an office, if he could get rich. He needed something that would drive itself, something that depended on a constant source of investment and return.

'Focus, Coyote, focus,' he urged himself. Focus on people close enough and the dung will emerge, he thought. Coyote was thinking of new products, cheap things to sell that people needed, like pet rocks, only cheaper. Maybe new games. Maybe his own line of furniture, like a tripod chair, portable, uncomfortable, cool-looking. Maybe a Swiss army knife, with gun, phone, shark-repellent, computer, and stove. Maybe a touch-thought holophone that would project an interactive holographic image of a screen and keyboard in the space before your eyes.

Or he could invent wide-spectrum glasses. He was thinking 'We are surrounded by things we cannot see. Radio waves, neutrinos, and death rays.'

Coyote understood that; he knew what it was like to swim in a sea of smells, to follow their special trails between the other smells. Coyote glasses would allow the observer to make any wavelength be visible or even all at once. It would be like being in the ocean deep, surrounded by rivers of information.

Then he knew. It would have to be computers, and the web, and it would involve the millions who visited the web like an outlaw town. It would be artistic and inspiring. He sat down to write the program, or rather the invitation to Termite who would write the program. All Coyote had to do was promise to help build a new mound. Coyote found a windowless building with a few cubicles and it was wired. Adding a coke machine and a candy machine, Coyote had finished preparations. This was going to work. And it did. Termite had written the perfect app.

Coyote invited Turtle over to see how it worked. "You enter your credit card number here and press go."

"But, won't it bill me?"

"Not if you don't use it, or if you forget to press the key to delay the daily autobilling. See how easy that is?"

"Sure. What is this page? What are these forms?"

"These are fractals that you put together to make your own art. Here, watch me buy a few and just assemble them, like so."

"I can't see them because of the ads."

"You can get rid of the ads by paying a small fee."

"Hey, there's one from Eagle, about living the Eagle way," said Turtle.

"Yes, the downside of capitalism. Anyone with money can buy an ad."

"So, where does the money go?" Turtle asked.

"To the Animal Orphan Fund. It's beautiful; it's run by Mother Possum."

"Wow, that's noble and good."

"Yes, it is. Here, press this button and the ads go away, for a small charge."

"Wow, okay, I can see all the frambles—

"Fractals. It's a sophisticated math program, you know."

"Okay, so what do I do with the fragals?"

"You put them together. Try."

Coyote watched Turtle poke and push, before interceding, "No, not like a tortoise shell. Look here."

"Those are people,"

"Yes!"

"And, they're mating with each other."

"Well, yes, but they don't have to. You make them mate with auto parts, donkeys, bottles, or clothing. That's the beauty of this—"

"But, it's pornography!"

"No, it's not. You just made it that way. It's art."

"But, there're only a few ways it can go together. Someone is always mating with someone, or something, else. That's disgusting!"

"What do you know, you're cold-blooded."

"I want my money back!" and Turtle leaned his shell against Coyote's nose.

"Of course, not everyone can appreciate art. Do you want to see some turtles and lobsters mating?"

"No, just the money refunded. All of it."

"Okay, no reason to be upset. Just fill out these forms and follow these easy to follow steps. Follow me?"

Turtle walked away without speaking. Coyote decided not to tell him that he forgot to press the 'not-buy' key to stop the automatic billing program.

Wakanda came in and asked, "What's wrong with Turtle?"

"Turtle was afraid of art."

"Maybe he's right. We should be afraid of art. We should be afraid of these toys, too," Wakanda said, as she swept her hand over the computers. "When it comes down to it the bottom-line, whatever, toys are inanimate. We can pretend, but eventually we learn to be like the toys, inanimate, deprived and isolated from life, real, living, breathing forms."

Coyote knew how important toys were, so he didn't answer.

He realized he needed to pinpoint a livelier species, maybe just mammals and he knew just the primates who would appreciate this— Monkeys! And, of course, humans. And, they did, and they paid. It was that simple.

Now, with his hard-earned, er, hardly-earned money he could have a new larger den. He hired Badger to dig it for him. Then, he invited Gopher Tortoise to design the interior.

Gopher Tortoise spoke: "Interior design is about people."

"Really, not shapes or functions?"

"No, people."

"Oh, please, Isn't everything about people?"

"It says so in literature, even children's literature, which reflects our society."

"Oh, please, it is the excrement from our digestive society. It used to be that a Desana maloca house was a womb for its people, and a Kwakwakawakw house ate its inhabitants. Now our whole culture eats the planet and excretes plastic toys. Wonder who gets to play with those?"

"So you want the earth-tone walls, with the cedar-bark floors?"

"Sure, okay."

"How can you afford me, by the way?" Tortoise asked.

"I started the Cancer Club for Men. I'm not just a client, I'm a doctor."

"Cancer?"

"Amazing food source, all we need to do is harvest it."

Otter came in and admired the spaciousness. He asked Coyote and Tortoise, "Why does wealth end up with a few? I mean, what makes them, how do they get rich? Not in bands or tribes, therefore it has to have something to do with agriculture, and the production of surplus."

Tortoise answered, "Maybe it is power law, when the number of links in a node doubles, then the number of nodes with doubled links decreases by 5 times. That could explain it."

"Not to me," said Coyote.

Coyote tried to explain wealth to Otter who came to visit.

"What are you wearing?" Otter asked.

"These? Oh, these are my Banker gang rags. It's a finance thing."

"I have my own research program," Otter announced.

"How can you do research?" Coyote asked.

"I call it the Bank America Torture Ceremony. I lure them in with the promise of free money. But it is basically a catch and release program to count and determine the health of humans," Otter explained.

Coyote said, "That is ridiculous, just look at them, see if they look healthy."

"That would not be scientific. I need the method and numbers."

"I never thought of you as a scientist," Coyote said with a little awe in his voice.

"Oh, anyone can be a scientist," Otter said.

"I know. I have a white coat myself."

"No, you have to follow the method. A number of individuals are captured, marked and released the same day. Then a week later a second sample is taken. Some individuals may be from the first sample. The total population can be calculated as the same proportion."

"Where did you learn that?"

"History Channel. It was used to estimate the human population of Paris, by LaPlace in the 1700s. Worked fine."

"It is an ugly flatscape," said Otter.

"No, a charming grassland," replied Coyote.

"How can you see that? It is nothing but dirt."

"There is charm in everything, from quarks to grains of dirt. You only have to be open so that it resonates with the charms from which you are built. Look at this pattern next to my paw. Can you design a pattern like that? Can you draw a trillion of them, all different, just in one patch of grass? Can we even appreciate the diversity?"

"Land is wealth," Otter declared, "but good forested land."

"Ideas are wealth," Coyote retorted.

"And, when you are out of ideas, how do you eat?"

"Ideas can find new things to eat, new unlimited resources, and then create a higher standard of life through money."

"Can you eat money?"

"Money is the source of virtue, and that lets us live faster and larger."

"What if you get too large?"

"We have to grow, otherwise we sit and die."

"What if you outgrow your house and die?"

"Not a problem, if new larger ideas can lead us to new larger houses."

"Growth makes things unequal and leads to bigger problems. Let me explain using this pie. Wealth is supply divided by demand. You want the pie to get bigger and bigger, so more people can have more pie. I think we have to reduce the number of eaters or reduce each piece of pie."

"Well, let's see, if I eat this big piece here—mmmm, that's tasty, is it blackbird or blackberry?—but then decide to eat another before Badger gets his share, then you're saying that Mouse has to get the crumbs, because we can't have a bigger pie?—mmmm, sweet."

Otter looked at Coyote's face smeared with fruits and crumbs, and just sighed, "It was cactus fruit pie, for Lutey."

Coyote found another crumb to snuffle up.

"After all, what is economics?" Otter asked academically, "It is just the study of how people use their surroundings, their house as it were, to meet their basic needs."

"Yea, well my basic needs include a Ferrari and a diamond watch," Coyote said.

"Every basic economy has to be based on sunlight and plants."

"The difference is," Coyote explained, "that I am rational and you are not. Economics has to be rational-based."

"If you were perfectly rational, then you could sell one of your balls or kidneys for thousands of dollars. Why don't you?"

"Thousands? Really? How much exactly? Oh, I suppose I need them."

"No, those are redundant organs. Don't need them both. The value of your body for parts may be easily $100,000."

"Where did you learn—never mind, Discover Channel."

"History Channel. But, you won't sell your healthy organs," Otter said. "Think about it this way. The cost of being alive often exceeds the cost of being dead. Am I irrational to want to be alive, even if it is costly?

Well?"

"Well," Coyote said, "obviously you are misunderstanding the prize winning economists who say differently." But, Coyote was calculating his fee of a $1000 for a kidney.

"Those guys are just Mercantilists, like you," suggested Otter. "I'm a capitalist, Otter. You are just one of those touchy, feely giver-awayers."

"You are not a capitalist, you are a crapitalist!"

"So, everything makes crap, that's why it's important."

"Yes, but we do not need to focus on it more than its worth or importance."

"Okay, then, crapitalism is the answer. It's a free market, anyone is free to crap. Besides, you're one to talk: You put your crap on rocks to act as road signs so the rest of us have to look at it."

"To take an ordinary subject and make it subordinary, that takes a crap-based imagination." concluded Otter.

"The meeting will come to order," announced Stinkbeetle.

"First, I have some good news. We have completed a merger with VeViN—for those of you not familiar with them, they are Verizonous Victims Nymous (they are not 'anon'), a group that meets to complain about telephone service. You should note that they are human, and—"

"Pardon me, Chair Stinkbeetle," interrupted Ben Willabunk, the VVN spokesperson, "but we are an action group, working against corporate inconsistency and unfair billing."

"Sorry, please, welcome to the meeting. We do already have a few human members, such as Trapper Bob over there. Can we accept the minutes from last week?"

"We have to kill Coyote permanently, for good," said Rabbit.

"Why?" asked Otter. "He can be good; he can help us."

"Wait, who's got the talking feather?" asked Crow.

"I do," Rabbit said. First, he held it with its back to the listeners and the inside curve to him, so he would hear his own words first; this would tame a harsh tongue. Then he turned the feather away from himself so the words could go straight to the others. "In the great medicine wheel, all animals are connected. Each animal is responsible to not grow too numerous and suppress the others. We know that, all except Coyote, and of course, humans. The wheel has to roll over Coyote now. I ask that we vote decide."

"No, Rabbit is right," nodded Crow. "Coyote has no understanding of tragedy and his blundering creates more of it. Being immortal, he has no idea of the preciousness of the script between the bookends of nothingness. I vote to flatten his highness."

"But, Turtle is immortal," Otter noted. "Wolf is immortal. Should we kill them, too?"

"Otter has a point," said Rabbit.

"Maybe, it's just that Turtle and Wolf have suffered. They know not to trick for fun or to kill for a thrill or out of irritation."

"Yes," said Eagle for the first time. "Coyote does not know what it is to die. He is not aware of his limits, the limits of fading away, even from memory."

"But, he is my friend," said Otter.

"Well, friends can die. Coyote will not weep for you when you die, because he does not understand death," Eagle pointed out.

"Yes, he does understand death. He has lost pups."

"Not enough," hissed Rattlesnake. "He needs to lose more."

"I will not be a part of this," said Otter and left.

Rattlesnake started to glide after him, but Eagle put a talon on his thin butt, and said, "Let him go. Even if he tells Coyote, Coyote will not listen. We should not hurt those who display such loyalty."

Rattlesnake pulled away, started to coil, then realized the wisdom of Eagle's words, "Yes, you are right. I have no quarrel with Otter. But, how can we dispose of His Trickiness properly?"

"I haaavve some thoughts on that," began Horse. "I am not the stupid hooooffer that he thinks I am." And he shook his head so his mane billowed. "No matter what we do, and we have done some dramatic killings of coyote, with shot guns and rocks, Coyote can come back to life if Fox jumps over him—or even a single hair of him. We need to kill Fox first."

"No, Fox is one of us. And, of all of us, he has suffered the most. No, we cannot kill him," judged Eagle.

"He is the little brooootther of Coyote. He—" snorted Horse, spraying mucus all over Crow, who flew up to a low branch and started preening.

"Thanks for the grease. Listen I know you are upset, but we need to focus on His Dogginess hisself. I think I know a way," and Crow paused dramatically and pulled out a bent feather. As it floated to the ground one of the little parasites on it started to make a suggestion, but nobody heard it, except for a few of the parasites on him, who were deafened by the volume. Crow continued, "We don't have to kill Coyote forever, just for a very very long time."

Rabbit and Eagle nodded.

"We just take a lesson from the humans and bury him for a long time. Out of sight out of mind. Fox depends on random motion to restore Coyote. If the evidence is buried deep enough, it may take a long time for Fox to know or guess or jump by accident."

"Will it work?" asked Horse.

"I think so," said Eagle, "We only need to try it. We'll need a good trap and a big hole. Let's get to work."

"I can do the hole," volunteered Bob, still smarting at his treatment by Coyote. "One of you will have to lead him to it."

The others hissed or neighed their agreement and willingness. "It's time for Coyote to move on. He was at his peak in the bronze age—" said Crow.

"No, Lead Age," suggested Rabbit. And they both laughed heartily.

"You know Foxes in Siberia, at a fur ranch, were bred for being tame. After a few generations of breeding for tolerance of humans, they were more social with people, but other traits began to appear, such as barking instead of growling, holding their tails high instead of low, perking their ears forward instead of backwards, and playing more—essentially juvenile behaviors."

"Why are you telling me this?" Fox asked Coyote.

"Because I heard this, and realized that people can domesticate wolves and fox, but they could never domesticate a Coyote."

Fox sighed and said in a low tone, "I want to kill myself."

"But, animals cannot kill themselves!"

"Sure they can, just look at Housemouse. He just stood still when Hawk came down. That was suicide."

"No, more like youth."

"I still want to die," Fox announced.

"Hey, why not masturbate to death," suggested Coyote always trying to get into the flow of conversation and be helpful.

"I was thinking games computer games."

"Hey, same thing," Coyote trumpeted.

"Yea, games, I would starve and waste away, yet I could change my mind later, not too late, but ..."

"Starvation. Now, there is a good idea. Just stop eating. That will give you plenty of time to straighten out your affairs and even change your mind if you need to. Then I could bring you some good mice and test your resolve. If you were too weak, it would take a lifetime to kill yourself by starvation. Feel better now?" Coyote asked cluelessly.

Fox rolled his eyes and sighed, "Humanity is the beast with a billion mouths, all open, a billion backs, all humping. Arrgghhh, I cannot fight it anymore," said Fox.

"See a change of topics is always going to cheer you up. Want to chase up a few mice?" Coyote asked, but Fox had gone.

The next day, Coyote came upon the body of Fox, lying on the bank near a bend of the creek. Fox had drowned himself, apparently. Coyote did not want Fox's death to be in vain; he wanted to do the right thing by his friend. He called many people to see Fox's body. Coyote tried desperately, using all his wily skills to convince the people he possessed supernatural powers. He was thinking to himself, 'If I revive Fox I will be even more famous.' He stepped over Fox three

times, and just as he was stepping over the fourth time, he pushed Fox
with the tip of his claw to make it appear the body moved.
He announced loudly, "Oh, look, my people, I made Fox come to life.
Did you not see him move?" But the people paid him no attention.
He threw his voice so it appeared to come from Fox's body,
"Hey, I am alive. Thanks, Coyote, for bring me back from death. You're
a great shaman. Really."

Some of the people paused a moment, but
one of them saw Coyote's mouth move. So, they keep walking away.
Coyote hooked a line on Fox's foot. Looped it around a boulder
and scuffed dirt over it. He called them back, and while they were
looking at Fox, he pulled the rope and Fox's body started to crawl
awkwardly. But, dust made Turtle sneeze and the rope was revealed.

"Aawwww," Coyote said as people walked away again.
Rabbit commented, "If Coyote is a shaman, there is nothing he
cannot do. He can peek in our secret souls, bring rain, raise the dead,
get good luck, make war, and predict the future. What can we do?"

"Wait til he proves he's a shaman," suggested Turtle.

Coyote brought a mouse to Fox, in case he was faking it. When the
mouse stayed uneaten, Coyote began to worry. Without Fox, he
was vulnerable to permanent death. He had to revive Fox, for real.
He remembered that Wolf had brought Otter back to life. Now, he
needed to convince him to do it again.

Wolf was resting near the log over his den, when he saw Coyote.
He groaned and rolled over.

"Mighty Wolf, noble Wolf, Fox has fallen
to the civilized sickness, Can you help him?" Coyote begged.
"No."

"NO? It's FOX, not some mouse or deer. Please, I'll do
anything!" Coyote pleaded for his little brother.

Wolf tried to bring Fox back by circling him three times. Nothing
happened. Wolf sat and thought for a long time. He told Coyote to
get him a bow and arrow, which Coyote stole from Target. Wolf shot
the arrow into the ground under Fox, who moved a little and groaned.

Wolf was adamant that this was the last time ever, "EVER!"
Coyote never did admit what he had to do to convince wolf
to perform the miracle. Fox went away for a while.

Coyote was strolling along the creek thinking how all the other animals had it easy. Coyote had tried to be like ant, storing food for winter, but he ate it all on the first cool day.

Coyote had tried to be a young salmon, facing upstream, with his mouth open, waiting for anything to come downstream, but he filled up with water.

Coyote had decided to imitate bear, but that was at the end of winter and all he had to eat was bark and bitter sap.

Now, Coyote was thinking the chigger lifestyle might be good, or maybe a cow would have an easier—

Suddenly he tripped on a root. He lay nose down on the ground and saw some pretty threads in the dirt. "Hey, who are you?"

"Fungus, Mike Fungus."

"Oh, you are low."

"We fungi network everything in soil. We link trees to trees and grass to trees. We're like, you know, a superorganism!"

"Superfungi?"

"You got it, pal."

"Do you think I could?"

"No, too small, too thick. But, have you thought about being a tree? We could work together as partners."

Coyote wondered.

Coyote was so tired. North America used to be so quiet, just a few people-eating monsters and a few tired gods. Now, it was like the intersection of two galactic highways. Was he going to have to contend with every single being that thought it was supreme?

Coyote noticed a tree laden with seeds, too many, so he knew it must be dying. He saw an opening in the trees, and recognized it as the local snake-sunning area, so he was careful to walk around it. After he had walked a while he had to pull over to piss. He found a small cedar and let loose.

"Hey!"

The exclamation startled him and he sprayed his right front foot.

"That's disgusting. Move down-root, would you?"

Coyote looked around for the speaker of these words, pushing the small tree aside to see better.

"Hey, that's amazingly rude of you."
Coyote focused on the sapling in front of him, the voice seemed
to be coming from it. He released his paw and the tree swayed back
across the vertical then back until it was upright.

"Quit pushing me!"
"I, uhh,"

"What, you can't talk cedar?"

"Sorry. Hey, teach me your
woody lifestyle. What would I have to do?"

"Well," said Cedar,
flattered that someone thought he had a good life, "move over there
about one cedar-length. Now, put your lower boles together. Extend
your roots down into the soil. Spread your branches. There, good."

Coyote stood straight, but not too. Held his arms out
and worked his toes into the soil, "Okay, now what?"

"Be flexible. Pull in the light and air from your branches, lift water
from your roots. How's that feel?"

"I can't get the water to go up. Maybe I should be teaching
you how to jump," Coyote noted sarcastically.

"Turn your branches
90 degrees so less water evaporates. Send those rootlets deeper."

Coyote tried, and stood there. The sun felt warm.
He dozed and soon fell over.

Cedar whistled a little tune through his needles.
Treeing was not for everyone.

Coyote wrote a love poem to Wakanda
   "Your eyes by monitor light
   fill me with information ...
    Your butt shadowed on the wall
    empties me with deformation—"
She froaned, in appreciation, Coyote expected.
 "So, what is this maskbook site you're looking at?" Coyote asked her.
  "Facebook."
      "Whatever, gahh. Should be called assbook."
Over her shoulder, Coyote read how Facebook promoted itself:
"Facebook gives people the power to share. It makes the world more
open and connected. Over 100 million people use Facebook everyday
to keep up with friends, upload an unlimited number of photos, share
links and videos, and learn more drivel about the people they meet."

Alone, Coyote browsed the users and clicked on women with less
clothing. Then he spotted an interesting one, "Madprofessor." He
started reading:

Rathgar's Details
Here for: Networking, Dating, Serious Servitude
Orientation: future
Body type: Ectomorphic (Slim, except belly)
Ethnicity: Caucasoid (head only)
Zodiac Sign: Cerberus
Smoke/Drink: Yes / Yes enthusiastically
Children: Love kids, want to make one or two from parts
Education: College graduate, Heidelberg Tech
Occupation: Geneticist, somatic engineer
Movies: The Sound of Music, Texas Chainsaw Massacre
Heroes: Frankenstein, Moreau, Bush

Rathgar's Thoughts
I feel screaming is an important part of legitimate research; it adds an emotional
content that you rarely find in science, and that seems to be important.
 I believe, and this is a certifiable true belief, that opera is one of humanities
highest accomplishments. Voices raised to a high volume bespeaks of the
harmony of human relations. However, raised voices by amps, such as rap or
heavy metallic music, are abominable to the 11th degree.
 I know that I smoke and drink too much, but these are stress-related
reactions. My research is world-altering and therefore puts much pressure. I
would like to try intercourse as a way of reliving stress, but, well, that is why I
am advertising myself on this site. I am as good with my fingers as I am with a

scalpel. I can tie knots with each hand simultaneously behind my back.

I do have some visual challenges that seem to have resulted from the blinking lights of my computers, as well as from staring into the discharges of my generators during novovivisynthesis experiments, but dark sunglasses help that. I am aware that my flowing white hair makes me seem older than my 30 years, but my skin is smooth and I am considering dying my hair red.

That could be Dr. Spicer for all he knew. One of the raves was from 'Mad scientist,' so Coyote followed the link there and read, 'We're DOOMED! Global warming puts—' —enough of that. Then he looked at the profiles of more women/girls with graphics and notes, starting with 'skreem kween.'

SKREEM KWEEN's Details
Status: Single
Here for: Networking, Dating, Serious Relationships, Friends
Orientation: Bi
Body type: Slim / Slender
Ethnicity: White / Caucasian
Zodiac Sign: Scorpio
Smoke/Drink: Yes / Yes
Children: Love kids, but not for me
Education: College graduate, Manatee Community
Occupation: Animal breeder

Skreemie Notes
And you only wished you lived it... I'm pretty easy going, If a fool don't fuck with me. I don't trust easily, if at all,there is very few people I will trust with anything , those select peeps know who they be.
I dig every single B-rated/Shitty ass horror movies . Fuck shit. even the good effect ones I dig. I just love blood , Gore , It's such a turn on. Yeah I'm a little twisted,it's what makes skreem kween Her.
I smoke , and I love it, my diet is smokes and caffine.It works wonder's and keeps me up at night ... Werd B! I'm a savage.
I have nightmares,All the time,I should be a fucking novilist or someshit with all the fucked up shit I dream about. I have anxiety issues, as well I get super nervous easily. Aspecially around large groups of people and situations I feel uncomfertable in. Which is why I keep dope people around me all the time.
I've been down for a long ass time, Im sick of these little shits going on about how They have soo much merch da da da... that it makes them more down.
SHUT THE FUCK UP PIPSKWEAKS FORREEEAAAAAAAAAAAL.
I listen too metal,undergroun.... anything and everything I can relate too. No I'm not an emo bitch. everyone needs music they can relate too.
IF YOU ADD ME, TALK/MESSAGE/COMMENT. thanks.

Oct 20 2008 10:09 PM, from Roberto
hey whats up girl thanks 4 tha add i like tha pic of u whats ur name my name is robert hit me back

Jan 31 2009 8:21 AM, from Bunny Hop
just a buncha top secret bunny bidness!! orderin sum mo bunny energy drinks
and merch! do u gots any carrot cake fo a bunny?? huhuuhuhuhh??
ill crunch! crunch! crunch! in yo face fleshy!!!! wuz da bizniz iz??????

Here was a hot picture from Zeala. He clicked over.

"Life is as good as you want it to be!"
Female, 24 years old, LAKE MARY, Florida, United States

Zeala Details
Status: Single
Here for: Networking, Dating, Serious Relationships, Friends
Orientation: Bi
Body type: 5' 3" / Slim / Slender
Ethnicity: White / Caucasian
Religion: Christian - real
Zodiac Sign: Virgo
Children: Someday
Education: In college
Income: Less than $30,000

Zeala's Blurbs
About me:
First off, I'm not gonna write about what a good person I am and how lucky
you'll be to have me as a friend and/or have a chance to know me, and what
a good-hearted, generous, trustworthy soul I am. Instead I'll write about my
way of philosophy and see if we share it. WARNING!!! Not suited for people
with quick temper, closed minded, who can't understand the bigger meaning
and can't read between the lines.... "I don't really like talking about me much
because I'm not self-absorbed, shallow, and superficial. Yeah, that's what I think
about people who all they wanna do is talk about themselves and what they've
done during the day every minute of it, with every little borring detail. I don't
trust people who have their own picture on their cellphone's wallpaper - I think
they're so absorbed with their own amour propre, are egoists, and all they care
about is themselves. I analize people a lot. You may not agree with me, that's
your own right, but I know it's true. Oh, and what's up with you people taking
pictures of yourself up close with your sunglasses on? What? I'm supposed
to guess what brand they are? Cause if you think you look better with your
sunglasses on on every single picture of yours - You Are Wrong - it makes you
silly and unattractive; cause if you are hiding your eyes - there is a reason behind
it, you need the big glasses to cover your ugly futures or are with a very weak
personality and are self-conscious, have your own self-criticism, have low self-
esteem and are trying to hide it all that behind the sunglasses. So, if you have
your sunglasses on on more than 50% of all your pictures STOP reading further.
I'm serious - STOP! Click the BACK button." –
   To Continue.... I guess the most important think about me is that I'm dead
honest, you ask me something - I'll tell you the truth straight to your face, even

if it will hurt your feelings. Some people think I'm joking or even lying when I'm straightforward with them, that's because those people (I found out later) have lied to me (thinking I'll never know the truth, but I always do eventually, sometimes too late) and can't process through their mind that I say the truth as is. (For some reason when I break up with a boyfriend, after a few months everyone just wants to tell me about him; how he has cheated on me, with who, where, and all the details. This comes even from the mouth of people I don't even associate with. They just come to me and start blabbing about him without me even bring him up and don't stop until they've said it all. I just wonder why is that? Why people rush to tell you all that when you just start to move on? They deliberatly want to hurt me, get me upset? People are just cruel.)....

One other thing about me is that I always boost people's confidence, which I now consider a bad trait and am working/trying to refrain from it. I say that because people find me when they are depressed and/or have a very low self-steam and need a friend. I try to help them see the positive side of life, telling them all the good fuitures they posses and comparing them to others, I sometimes really exaggerate aspecially when it comes to their looks and that's where I go wrong - they always believe it and become very cocky and superficial. I'm just trying to comfort them, not to give up that life is beautiful, but instead their ego skyrockets. And the funny thing is (I'm talking about women) that they start to think they are so beautiful and sexy, they've become to think they are way better then me and to prove it to themselves they stick a knife in my back. Trying to bring me down with words to make me self-concious, spreading untrue rumors, stilling my dreams (goals) and rubbing it in my face that they've succeded faster then me. That's why never tell anybody your plans or a goal and how you'll achieve it because people steal that, seriously. Such small minded women, I pitty them, they are so pathetic. No matter how much you help a person, he/she never appreciates it. The thing is I don't care if you never say "Thank You" to me, but when you see me show some respect, that's all I ask for.... I'm a very down-to-earth person and I know I'm beatiful inside, but never outside, I just think of myself as attractive - more or less.

'Won't she ever shut up?' Coyote wondered, and skipped a few pages.

What I'm trying to say is that I've had a few dissapointments in life as I'm sure everyone has, but that don't make me a victim, but a winner. I forgive people, but I never forget. So, thank you to all you backstabers, liers, cheaters, users, players, cause now I know how to spot you and protect myself.

<u>Who I'd like to meet:</u>
Straight, Gay, Bi, Tri and in between people. Women: 21-28 years old; Men: 24-31 years old; Others: 21-31 years old. I'm putting the age preference because I know people between those ages I'll have more in common with. So if you are 50 something over and you bother me to tell me how much I'm missing on, don't waste your time writing me - i know exactly what I'm not missing. I don't lack the guidance of older men - I have 2 grandfathers, a father, an older brother, and many couisins. You can't teach me anything- don't want to learn. And if you tell me that guys my age are loosers and can't satisfy me like you can - I'll tell you that YOU ARE THE LOSER and just because you

got some Viagra doesn't make you the Big Man. And because you can't find someone your own age, you have to prey upon the youngsters so that you can boost your sad ego to feel younger. I say all that because no matter what I write, there are always sad desperate old men harrasing me. Maybe cause they know they'll NEVER score with me, no matter how much money they got. Old is old. Young is young. I'm still young and prefer young people close to my age. But hey old man, don't give up, I'm sure there are plenty of young women who lacked father attention in their early teen years looking to fill that big hole of lost father's love/attention. Yeah. I think women attracted to old men have serious unresolved issues and old men dating young girls who can be their daughter (when counting the age difference) I call pedophiles. There I said it. And the commment "love has no age limit" is crap. That's for stupid and naive people to believe. However, if we say it's true for instance, then why don't you You old bag find some woman 20 years older than you (ex. you'll be 55 and she'll be 75, tho I can't see any diff) Hey, Love has no age limit right? So, why we never see that pair? Correct me if I'm wrong, please, but I personally never heard of such pair. If you tied the young man in his 20s, I guess it's possible then, but no 50something year old man we'll choose old.

Coyote started tapping frantically to add this woman to his list. Of course he would have to knock 10,000 years off his age. Not a problem. He reached for a Leo DiCapricorn mask. Then he saw the comment by Kaiser and decided to check him out first for some clues on what to write for himself.

Kaiser Helmut
Male, 31 years old, Doppelganger, Texas, United States

Interests

General	I like movies, music, and to draw, I am an out doors kinda guy who loves being in nature
Music	I've gotten really into a foriegn music faze, bands like Nightfish, and my personal fav, Within Temptation
Movies	I try to watch them all, but tend to prefer the older ones to the newer rehashed remakes
Television	don't watch tv
Books	anything by Terry Brooks or Ann Macafree
Heroes	my grandfather

Kaiser's Details

Status:	Single
Here for:	Friends
Orientation:	Straight
Hometown:	White Settlement, Idaho
Body type:	5' 10" / Slim / Slender
Ethnicity:	Native American
Religion:	Agnostic
Zodiac Sign:	Minus

Smoke/Drink: No / No
Education: Some college

I'm about 5'10" and 168 lbs., semi-long brown hair, blue-green eyes, with a
normally quiet personality, but I can easily get loud and wild
Who I'd like to meet: Michelle Rodriguez, Wes Craven

His weapons: His hands and muscles. Gatlings.
His cars rides: Corvette
His armors: ?
His properties: Beacon St.

Nov 7 2008 7:09 AM
You inspire me.
Keep up the good work. Thank you :-)
I would like to share a couple of inspirtionl quotes:
Feel free to share them with others especially if they are facing obsticles or need
a boost of encourgement.
1) God did not bring you this far to leave you.
2) Through God all things are possible. (Just ask me, and Obama lol)
3) This is the day that the lord has made. Let us rejoice and be glad in it.
4) Things are getting better. Keep the faith.
Have a bless and joyous day :-)
~Meredith~

Boring, but Coyote decided to go see this Meredith.

"I had to delete some 400+ crazies from my page… If you feel like you were
deleted in error toss me a friend request otherwise… Stalk on! Kiss-Kiss… ☒
ME!"

Female, 30 years old, Wherever the good Lord takes me, Arizona, United States

About me:
I'm a PROUD CHRISTIAN WOMAN & MOTHER! I klnow I SHOUT
all the time, but I am Caring and PASSIONATE. I am LOVING ☒ and
Understanding. I am Intelligent… Both STREET SMARTS and Book
SMARTS. I am FUNNY and HAPPY :D Always!In my eyes I am just a
GIRL. I am HONEST † and FAITHFUL…. I am Trustworthy and can hold a
SECRET like no other. I am Simple and yet COMPLEX. I am the QUEEN
of Bad Hair Day's and NO Make-up. My GREATEST Strength is also my
Biggest weakness… I am a FORGIVING SOUL. I live each day to please no
man, but rather to Please THE Man… JESUS CHRIST Our LORD and
Savior. I am NOT Perfect however I am REAL and I am Random… and that's
what makes me… ME!
Who I'd like to meet: Good H E A RT E D Christian peeps! If your NOT
about the JESUS Juice and into the whole "Drama Queen" thing P E A C
E-Out Girl SCOUT!

Movies: Passion of The Christ, The Notebook, Dances with Wolves & Titanic.
Television: I don't watch T.V.
Books: The B I B L E!!!
Heroes: JESUS is my HOME BOY! And My Daughter!

Married ToTheMan's †'s Details
Status: Single
Hometown: Viola, ID
Ethnicity: Latino / Hispanic
Religion: Christian - other
Zodiac Sign: Plus
Children: Proud parent
Occupation: Cheerleader for the Gifted!

Viola Normal School
Viola,ID
Graduated: 1996
Student status: Alumni
     1992 to 1996

MarriedToTheMan's †'s Networking
Modeling - Model - Makeup
DIOR - Makeup Artist / National Events
Dance - Performance - Other
NFL Cheerleading / Gymnastics

Dances with Wolves, my ass, thought Coyote. More like Tangles with Termites. For a cheerleader, she had too many clothes and not enough cleavage. Everyone seemed to be slender and from Florida. But, this Mouse King seemed to like her. Mouse King might have some fruitful links.

Mouse King
"2nd place makes you the first loser"

Male, 36 years old, FORT LAUDERDALE, Florida, United States

Mouse King's Blurbs
What can I say, I am just an average guy. I am an extremely busy person, always on the go. I have a challenging career, which I enjoy very much. Appearance wise, a lot of people tell me that I look like Ralph Nader and some people tell me that I look like that guy from the TV show Prison Break. I guess if it were possible for the Prison Break dude and Nader to get together and have a baby it would probably look like me. Scary thought! Anyway, aside from all of that, I have been allocating a lot of my time towards fitness and bodybuilding. I have recently competed in my first show and had a respectable showing, but now I feel like I am armed with the knowledge that it will take for me to get to the next level. So 2009 will be a time for some serious training and really make an

impact in my next show. On my free time I enjoy going to the beach, going out with friends, traveling, and relaxing at home. I love to party, but an occasional movie night with a few drinks and friends suits me fine also. Of course since I work hard and have little free time, I like to play hard when given the opportunity. I think my friends would all agree with that statement. Speaking of friends, the friends who I have close to me mean a lot to me and I will do anything for them.

Mouse King's Interests
General   Working Out, MMA, Strong Man Contests
Heroes   Arnold S.

Mouse King's Details
Status: Single
Here for: Networking, Dating, Friends
Orientation: Straight
Body type: 6' 1" / Athletic
Biceps: 27"
Ethnicity: White / Caucasian
Zodiac Sign: Sagittarius
Smoke / Drink: No / Yes
Children: Undecided
Education: College graduate
Occupation: Corporate Real Estate/Pool Boy
Income: $100,000 to $150,000

Nov 6 2008 10:25 PM
Hey Bill!! A few of us are thinking about coming down that way this weekend on sat night for my birthday.
Let me know if you're gonna be around! :)
ISABELA

Nov 6 2008 5:00 PM
hello beautiful! good for knowing of you, desire you this good, besote great, hmmmmm finally she obtains to desire chayane (see me under 'Electra Sunrise')

She might be hot, so Coyote immediately followed the electronic scent to Chayane.

Electra Sunrise began singing at a very young age and pursued her love of music through out her adolescent years. She puts passion, effort and energy into her music that is rarely seen. Her versatility and experimentation with different types of music is what keeps this young artist motivated. As a result her music is an energetic blend of electro, pop, rap, big band, African, and urban music. Never willing to compromise her message of creative experimentation, her lyrics always surprise and contain depth and definition.
    Electra has always followed her own path, which is often the road less

traveled. She states: 'This is me, what you see is what you get...I would never let anyone create an image for me. I keep it real in hopes that you'll appreciate me for who I truly am. I'm doing what I want the way I want to do it.' This is just one of the aspects that separate Electra from the new crop of musical talents. 'A lot of times artists have to be formed,' says Electra. 'I'm still growing myself as an artist and I find it much easier to express how I feel in my music. I did not have to be shaped into who I am or the artist that I am becoming and filling up.' She spent the last couple of years writing and working long hours in studio developing her vision of where she sees her music heading.

Electra believes that everyone has something unique to bring to the table, 'As an artist i'm learning day by day who i really am and appreciate how music is playing a positive role in my life'. Her upcoming album, which is set to be released in the approaching months, contains many energetic tracks that will, 'certainly make you want to move and feel like you've never felt before'. This should be great news to her dedicated legions of myspace fans. On display will be her notable vocal abilities and the sweetness of her voice which is guaranteed to leave you wanting to hear more from this talented and sensual artist. She goes on to say, 'I would like to thank my family, friends and wonderful fans for the love and support they've shown me. Your support is what makes all the hard work and late nights bearable and worthwhile. If my music speaks to you personally and makes you feel good about yourself then I've accomplished what I've set out to do. Much love and appreciation to you all'.

Was she writing about herself? Who was writing? Was she two people? She was certainly beloved of Perry Player. Let's see ...

Perry Player
"Undereducated people should think before they speak or write...when u make an uneducated assessment about something u know nothing about just proves how ignorant u really are.. you fear nothing u have knowledge about. Like vampires—I know about 'em, so I don fear 'em."

TELL ME ABOUT YOURSELF - The Survey
Name: let me introduce myself my name is Poon Tang Dong Jr. the III
Birthday: May 33th 1975
Birthplace: in the back of J&B liquor store on Alter and Southampton
Current Location: I'm at the parkside projects come holla at me
Eye Color: deep shit brown
Hair Color: deep shit brown
Height: 4'12"
Right Handed or Left Handed: right to write left to pimp slap out of line hoes
Your Heritage: white trash,redneck,honkey,cracker
The Shoes You Wore Today: stink pink gators for my Detroit Playas
Your Weakness: big lips both sets :D (|) and big (.)(.)'s and (_!_)'s
Your Fears: getting cut off welfare
Your Perfect Pizza: xtra cheese onions,and anchovies
Do you think you are Attractive: like u even need to ask this question

Are you a Health Freak: no just a freak no health involved
In the past month have you gone on a Date: my bitches take me out every night
In the past month have you been on Stage: just once i was shaking what my
    mama gave me i made 55 dollars BALLIN!! don't hate cuz i know u are
Ever been called a Tease: everyday sorry i can't fuck everybody ..but i do try
Ever been Beaten up: everyday in middle school HATERS!!! mad cuz i had
    all the fly honeys
Ever Shoplifted: I'm a certified kleptomaniac if u need something hit me up
How do you want to Die: In a drive by shooting or in a plane on fire in
    a hurricane being hi jacked
What do you want to be when you Grow Up: a gynocologist it's been
    my dream since i was 3
Status: I sleep around with as many hot women as i can.i always like
    the game musical chairs when i was a kid now i like 2 play musical beds..
Here for: Stalking /fuck buddies/serious short term relationships 3 to 4
    weeks tops/giving hot rich pillow princesses the best orgasm they ever had..
    and i love strippers and getting lap dances..
Orientation: I love hottt women a lot =) preferably black women,but i don't
    discriminate cum 1 cum all or don't cum at all just PLEASE!
Ethnicity: Polish / Italian /and sometimes i think I'm black
Religion: Catholic non confirmed
Sign: Taurus May 33th I share the same birthday with Salvador Dali
    ,and Louis Farrakhan should give u a good idea of my personality.

Nov 7 2008 5:41 AM
baby go 2 bed!!!!! u all ready know i will..GO 2 BED!!!!
⊠⊠Mechelle⊠⊠

Nov 6 2008 4:23 PM
cuz i want to =P ill be gentle with the first bite!! Lmfao Sheila

Too bad he had the wrong equipment for Coyote. He tagged on to
Sheila.

~⊠ Sheila ⊠~'s Details
Status: Single
Here for: Networking, Dating, Serious Relationships, Friends
Orientation: Straight
Body type: 5' 2" / Slim / Slender
Ethnicity: White / Caucasian
Religion: Catholic
Zodiac Sign: Sagittarius
Smoke / Drink: No / Yes
Children: Proud parent
Education: Some college
Occupation: Accounting Manager, Wachovia

   ~⊠ Sheila ⊠~'s Companies

Walkoverya
Accounting/Office Manager
1984-Present

GOOD MORNING
HAVE A WONDERFUL DAY
LOTS OF HUGS!!!!!!!!!!!!!!!!!!
ELENI

Nov 1 2008 5:26 AM
Hi Sheila
I wish you to have a lovely weekend
I love you Johna Wayne

This could be the one, thought Coyote. Yes, her picture revealed an acceptable area of flesh.

Johna Wayne Buffett
I like beer and booze and boxing. I am an undercover nerd and I seek the same in my playmates. I enjoy late night insanity with my favorite girls and boys. I love Shakespeare's Sonnets. I like to lecture people as though I know what I'm talking about. I unintentionally offend people when I call them disillusioned, tree-hugging dorks. I don't like having my photo taken. I like it when people say "fixin' to" and "warsh". I hate the sound of fingers popping. I love to write. Birds and bugs scare me. I love Indians, feather and dot. I believe that I know EVERYTHING. I love Peter Sellers. I hate manchildren with Peter Pan Syndrome. I have an afinity for Peter Pan peanut butter. I have a special place in my heart for the term "tall, dark and handsome."
Who I'd like to meet: Little Richard; Black Francis; Anais Nin; Midget alchemists who kidnap people in the middle of the night; Bob Dole, Elizabeth Dole, Onada Dole; Lennox Lewis

Possums are assholes (view more)
I'm afraid of my mailbox (view more)
Credit Card company date rape (view more)
Not hispanic enough... a mutt bitches (view more)

‡ Johnna Buffett.
‡ Born in 83'.
‡ I ☒ PMS.
‡ I could spend the rest of my life listening to Bon Jovi Sing Me Love Songs.
‡ I ☒ Concerts.
‡ I ☒ Good Friends.
‡ I'm A Scorpio.
‡ I ☒ the ocean.
‡ I ☒ the stars.
‡ I'm more famous than you know.
‡ Dreaming is my favorite Adventure.

‡ I'm going to make the world fall in love with me.
‡ I'm a poet and a musician.
‡ I want to do something big with music.
‡ I love to sing in the shower.
‡ Always Chase your Dreams.
I am me.

Moody say something about you being just like him??? Unless your throwing people out of moving automobiles I THINK NOT!!!! He is so screwed in the head... no your not like him! But that would be entertaining if he actually said something like that, being that it is SOOOOOOOOOOOOOOO far from the truth!!!! The nerve of these EX's sometimes though HUH!! They take so much of our energy!! I say FUCK em all!!!!

Coyote wrote to her immediately, suggesting some new variations on old themes. Then he noticed a compliment by Neraka and decided to check her out.

NERAKA's Blurbs
About me:
If you don't know me, my name is Neraka. I am the single Mom of two great kids. If you do know me you know how proud I am of them in everything they do. The are extremely smart, protective of their Momma, giving, talented beyond my wildest dreams and their most important feature is that they still believe in people and the world. I can only hope that I taught them a little bit of that. I have dedicated my world to my kids and have done well, if I don't say myself, but they are now getting to the age where I can have a bit of a life of my own and I do want a life of my own. I work very hard to live comfortable and now I want to play just as hard. I am definately unique but very traditional.
Who I'd like to meet: I am using this space to post a thought. When I looked at My Space today I realized that I have been poked, kissed, I own a fucked up looking animal that I asked other people to play with and I have been bought a number of times... I DIDN'T FEEL A THING!!! The comments become more and more raunchy and the undertones are ones of infidelities, casual meetings (and I don't mean coffee), and future meetings that will probably never happen. WTF... I am one of them!!! When did that happen?? I realized that I had become addicted to watching people over the net. My life has become so driven to live comfortable that I don't have a social life anymore. I miss the days of going out and really speaking with people face to face... actually meeting people. I still chat frequently with a more than casual friend of my recent past, you know him as Butch. He has become my best friend in the world. I share a portion of every day of my life with him and we will always, always, always have that. It really doesn't matter who trys to step on that because guess what... it's not going to happen. He knows me inside and out and I him. We were together through some really trying times and decided to part but only only in living separately.

what up Johna! nice seeing up in Sacramento at the Cali Bash!!!

Looking Beautiful as Always!
diablito

liz i love you can you comment back

This was great her made a few suggestions to her and Liz to get back him at his tag, Bignoser. Now, just to wait for the hot responses. Within an hour, he had his first response. He eagerly opened it.

Bignoser:
You have been reported for behavior which violates the rules of conduct outlined in Facebook's Terms of Service. Reasons for this may include but are not limited to:
- Sexist, racist, or insulting remarks in our social applications
- Using the Facebook mail system to send spam or advertising
- Registering more than one unique user account
- Offensive or inappropriate pictures in your profile or albums
- Being an animal pretending to be human

In order to avoid having your account suspended you must read and agree to the terms outlined in our Code of Conduct by submitting the online form located at: http://reports-facebook.com/abuse-warning/user-agreement/terms_of_service2.htm You must then submit proof, such as photos, of your self-abasement.
Failure to submit this confirmation will result in the permanent disabling of your account within 24 to 48 hours.
Dawn Wishnice,
Facebook™ Dispute Resolutions

Coyote punched keys furiously and sent it to his new friends:

I got this email and i have never even talked to anyone who wasnt my friend to offend anyone!! And i only have one account!! I go to the site this "person" sent me and all i get is something not even doing with facebook. Anyone else get this? Wha?

Then, Coyote got excited and signed up for Twitter, myfacebook.com, spacebook.com, myface.com, and farcebook.

Refaced

Turning Green Or Fighting Global Fever

Coyote parked the hummer almost on top of the den
and crawled in to lie down.

"Dad, you shouldn't be wasting
and polluting so much by driving that thing," said Topkan.

Coyote was tired from driving all night trying to catch Rabbit,
but he was touched by the pup's interest, so he answered,
"I'm recycling it, after I liberated it from the rich."

"Dad, we need to be frugal and green."
"We must remember that Coyote was green first," Coyote started, "as
green as a tree frog—"

"Mom told us that story, about the bluebird,
pond, tripping, and shit."

Coyote's upper lip drew back, but he was too
tired to offer an educating bite to the young. Instead he curled up and
went to sleep. He was dreaming about Bluebird when he heard the
strange sound, "hhzzzackkkk," the sound of the sinus impaired. He
woke but no one else was around.

Coyote meanwhile was serious about ecology, about being green.
He thought, and slept and thought and slept, then announced
to his family, "Let the humans change their light bulbs and all shall be
harmonious. And let the animals do their parts, having fewer offspring
and keeping away from the human's crops. There, problem solved."
And he went to sleep again.

A dream came to him of a bluebird going to a pond. He woke and
raced out of the den, hopped in the hummer and coughed off.
When he got to his destination, Brown Lake, he parked under a large
tree, efficient predator that he was.

Pretty soon a female bluebird
bobbled by, hunting insects on the ground.

Coyote watched and calculated. As the bird turned from him then
dropped to catch a grasshopper, Coyote raced over and pinned her to
the ground, holding her down with one claw. He looked at her wings
and thought, 'how artistic of me to pin her this way,' then he spoke
softly, "Tell me, or I will eat you, where is the secret pond of blueness?"

The bird, named Vanity by her mate, said imperatively, "First, let me up and blow the dust off my feathers." Coyote automatically did that.

Vanity said, "Thank you, now catch me two grasshoppers to make up for—" Coyote raised a claw in threat, but Vanity said, "How rude. The pond is two kilometers east. I will go now." She flew directly up out of Coyote's range.

"What is a killo-meet-her?" Coyote asked.

She just pointed east; she too had heard the story of how Coyote got brown.

Coyote started trotting east, thinking that all he had to do was reverse the original instructions and he would be green again. When he saw the pond, he made himself trip and roll on the road, then got up and shook.

There seemed to be a few oil patches on his fur, but he figured that wouldn't matter. He dove in, then jumped out and in two more times. Careful not to trip this time, he stood in the late sun to dry. When he saw his paw was green, he raced back to the hummer and home.

"Wow, dad, cool, super, look at you!" said Topkan.

Coyote nodded in acknowledgment, but then Wakanda screamed, "What happened? Are you okay?"

Coyote was confused, but said, "Hey, I'm green again, that's all."

Wakanda, said, "No, that's not all. Look in my mirror."

Coyote went to her room and groaned at what he saw. He was patchy. His two front paws were green, there were brown patches on his back and sides, green patches on his tail, blue patches on his chest and belly and one back paw, and the rest was white. He slumped to the dirt.

His mate patted him on the head. "What did you do?" she asked.

"I tried to become green again, like I used to be. Rolled in the dirt, then bathed three times in the pond."

When Wakanda heard where the pond was, she groaned. "That is an acid pond, now, from the concrete works. Somehow the water affected different parts of you, bleached some of your fur."

Coyote answered, "No problem, I'll just try another pond later."

It did not work. The next bluebird pond made no changes. The pups were having fun in the water. Coyote looked at them, almost as big as he was now.

Xegwe said, "It's okay. We think it's cool."

Coyote nodded and was thoughtful, maybe he could make a flag to match, white, with a blue earth and white clouds and green forests. It could be the Natural Coyographic Society flag, and he would lead the movement to save the earth from hummers and waste.
He would fly everywhere to be worshipped as the savior of—

"Hey, dad," observed Zora, "there's some brown coming out of your Amazon region."

Yoniatario said, "What about all the traveling, moving around, mixing up things, isn't that bad?"

"Hey, ecotrips. I know. Been there, done that. Time to move on, maybe develop an ecospirit," Coyote ruminated, lifting a blue paw.

Crow was watching this and thought, 'He's a lo-cal loser trying to be a glo-balling saint,' not realizing how prophetic it might be.

The figure moved slowly from the shadows in the laboratory,
a misshapen hand clutching a test tube. Coyote gasped,
then sighed, as Dr. Spicer stepped into the pool of light
from a desk lamp.

        Coyote said, "I thought you'd be grosser. In hiding?"
Spicer was a pleasing figure of medium height with a stripe of grey
at each temple; his hands were delicate.

        It must have been a trick of the light, or the mind,
Coyote thought.

        "I'm fine, never better, three bowls of fiber a day
and I'm as regular as old faithful. Why, I—"

        "But, the scandal at the college. You, I, we—"

"Not much of a problem. Seems there is no such thing as bad
publicity. You were the only proof, and you blew town," and Spicer's
eyes narrowed, "Why *are* you here by the way?"

        "I just wanted to stop by and say hi, for old times sake.
You noticed my cool four-color fur? What are you working on?"

"Oh, I'm glad you asked. Remember the K9-site, that gave us so
many problems? Let you show you."

        Spicer and Coyote reconnected, and it
turned out that Spicer needed an experimental subject for a few new
techniques, so he pointed to the fur and asked Coyote what he might
want in terms of new characteristics.

        "I want to be a dire wolf, giant
panther, massive snake, huge toad, giant mosquito. I want everything
gigantic. Monstrous, Enormous."

        "Just like Tawis-karong, I suppose."
"Who?"

        "Just a myth. Never mind."

        "Could a Dire Wolf kill a bison?"

"I suppose. You know, what you really want is a singular hunter,
like a running bear."

        "A bear, no, not one of those."
"Think about it, these running bears, or short-faced bears, were pursuit
predators. Imagine a grizzly that could run 50 miles an hour."

        "Hmmm. What happened to them?"
"They died out about 11,000 years ago, climate change probably
caused them to overheat."

Coyote decided to go more for appearance and strength this time.
After all, he was clever and had to trade off the secondary
characteristics, like the poor appetite choice of the horse or
the brittleness of kestrel bones. He was fixated on the dire wolf as
a solution, whose large bones would offset any secondary weakness.
What else would work? The colors of a tropical fish, yes. The penis of
the horse, of course, but more retractable. So many possibilities.

Spicer decided to use light to stimulate the changes this time,
much more direct, much less painful. "We know the tool kits of
developmental genes are the same for all animals. Take the Hox
proteins or the Pac-6 master body builder."

"What, an exercise thing?"
"Never mind," Spicer said as he was pointing to his diagrams.
"The difference is in how the kit is used."
"What shall we call the new me?" Coyote asked.
"I was thinking Teras Bulbous, heh, heh, heh," giggled Spicer.
"What? What's that mean? The Mongol?"
"More like mongoloid. The crucial thing is that the *environment* trips
those genes on; that is where the secondary characteristics can be
triggered or suppressed, also."

Coyote nodded cluelessly.
"Listen, I need to have one of my colleagues work on this with me.
Although I am a certified, renowned genius, unlike those academic or
corporate idiots, I need to have a younger perspective with some of
this stuff. She has new skills and new techniques. I want you to meet
Dr. Kornfellow, Lisa Kornfellow of the Plundercamp Institute."

"Pleased to meet you, sir," and she smiled.
Coyote wondered if she knew of his animal history with Splicer,
then blurted, "Is she a Spicer girl?"

"How do we get this to happen?" she asked.
"Well—" Coyote started.
"Shut up! That's an academic question. We use a genetic switch,
like the kind that has been driving evolution since the Cambrian.
Look, in some animals the mouth develops from the blastopore, so it
can be anywhere on the body—"

"You mean I could have another mouth on my shoulder?"
"Where the mouth is separate from the blastopore opening, as in
most vertebrates—"
"I want the shoulder mouth!"
"—like flies and mollusks. I don't think you want another mouth.

110

Wouldn't you rather have a large cutting claw on your front legs? We could do that."

"You mean like a dinosaur?"

"Velociraptor, yes. I think it would be safer if we did not try new genes at all. We need to be safer this time. Actually, it should be easier, because we are going to just shift the geography, that is the zones, of the genes. The themes are set and tested; all we want to do is make small variations."

"Hmm," Coyote fell asleep with his eyes open.

"We're just going to study the new environment, as it is, and make micro-expansions to exploit the new ecological opportunities of living with machines in the cities. I think we should look at the crayfish, the—"

"What!?" Coyote woke up.

"—the Swiss army knife of undersea adaptation. Look, two kinds of antennae, two kinds of claws, maxillipeds, pleopods."

"I don't want peds and pods. I want sophisticated weapons. Besides, I like to eat crayfish; I hunt them in the creek; they are small and crunchy good."

"You saw the movie, Spiderman?"

"Yea, so?"

"The spinnerets for making silk are just a modification of a gill branch of an appendage."

"I don't have gills," Coyote noted.

"Perhaps we could model one from a lung. I want you to think about it, the advantages of it. You could traps animals in a web. Look, you obviously have mutations already, since you can talk. Ever heard of the FOXP2 gene?"

"No, shouldn't it be called the CoyoteA1 gene?"

"It may play a role in the origin of language; it had only been found in rodents, and of course humans."

"Rodents! Oh, no, Mouse or Rabbit?"

"Rabbit. How did you know? Discovery channel?" asked Kornfellow.

"Big Bob's Bathroom Reader, I think it was."

Spicer was pacing as he was thinking out loud, "Well, we know that animals pass their genes vertically to their offspring. And, we know that bacteria can force horizontal transmissions of their genes within one generation. So we are basically putting Coyote in a horizontal network and use Staphylococcus to transfer the genes from the lab to Coyote—that means no more shots, all without sacrificing time or efficacy."

"Brilliant, the bacteria get sex without reproduction and Coyote gets the changes. Of course, we are creating a new megaspecies of bacteria to carry the changes. What could happen if some other animal gets, ah, 'infected'?"

"Well, I expect that it would be like a book of recipes, that without the ingredients being present in the environment, would mean the new carrier organism could not make a dinner."

"Could happen with Coyote?"

"Perhaps, perhaps."

"The addition of photosynthesizing green bacteria is going to make coyote into a plant-animal?"

"Actually, a FlAP, I suppose, Fungus-like Animal Plant."

"So, Coyote will be domesticating these new bacteria?"

"Or they him possibly. I think it is an important advance in symbiosis. Mammals have too long remained at a low potential for symbiogenesis. Coyote will be the first to advance."

"Brilliant, sir, brilliant," Lisa brownnosed, "what else do you plan?"

"Well, I noticed wood fibers in his dung. I have no idea why, unless he thinks he is a termite. But, that gave me an idea. I think I have ways to streamline his system and make it an optimally efficient processor. For example, all that urine and dung is a waste. The urine alone is a rich soup of unused nutrients. If I simply add an 'xxx' microbe to his system, the waste would be used to generate more energy."

"About the chlorophyll?"

"Yes, I know. The green bacteria is going to have to be tied to guard hairs on his back, otherwise, heh, heh, he might have to lie on his back with his legs spread to get charged."

"Ha, ha, that is pretty funny image. Let's get back to work. I have a new combination to test."

Coyote was lying on his back with his legs spread, soaking up the sun and groaning with pleasure, letting his dinner of mice digest and dreaming of using his new genetic changes to impress some foxes. If only the secondary characteristics could be suppressed.

Dr. Spicer had his own following, a group from Anima, who held signs that said 'abusive to animals' and 'needless and silly.'

He avoided them, disguised as a student with torn jeans and sweatshirt.

"What did you want to see me about, Lisa?"

"I want to add a blue fluorescent protein to the mix to study stem cells."

"After the Korean research? The French used a jellyfish gene. They injected into embryos. We would have to inject into the blood or muscle at multiple locations."

"But, it should help us track shifts."

"Epidermal only or total saturation? Saturation would be too slow at his age."

"Who is doing glow-in-the-dark beer?" Lisa asked.

"Where does this fit in the scheme of things?"

"It's part of the technology RING."

"Ring?" Spicer asked.

"Robot Info Nano Genetic. Technology has turned inward now, from the environment to the mind and genes."

"No, nonsense, we have faster planes and trains."

"Not much faster, not—" Lisa noted.

"Maybe because we are more fit?"

"It's a funny kind of fitness, fake fitness. We are adapting ourselves to fantasies, not to predators or droughts. It will be virtual until the drought dries out our sinuses and the heat toasts our synapses. We replaced a real economy with a virtual screen. Technology isn't speeding up, it's turning inward, so it just seems faster.

"Where is it going?" Spicer asked.

"We're accelerating downhill now. It's not just a trend it's a deep, narrow chreod. We're *doomed*."

"Hey, wanna make it with me?"

"Yea, sure," Lisa said, toying with a curl above his ear.
The two lab coats twirled and writhed with passion.

As they lay on the floor smoking new cigarettes, with SafeSmoke,™ Spicer noted: "We are not just selecting one desirable feature; we are getting many gene interactions in a whole living organism."

"So what?"

"So, we have to take the bad with the good, because we cannot isolate anything. By the way, how did you solve the penis problem?"

"Had to use an electrobiomechanical solution; implanted a servo to extend it from 4 inches to 28 inches, then retract it when he needed to run—"

"How did you solve the problem skin elasticity?"

"Elasticity? Hmmm, I think it's in my notes. Let me see, hmmm, oh, here. This is important, what about transfer? Is he going to burn up or collapse?" Kornfellow asked with concern.

"The environment will constrain his new changes. The changes will all turn off, if his energy falls below a minimum level."

"Brilliant, sir. This is Nobel frontier stuff," Kornfellow congratulated Spicer, "Let's bring him in, now."

Coyote could tell that sex had been performed recently in this room. He started to sniff the closest crotch, but Kornfellow boffed him with a handfull of files. Coyote smelled food on the lab counter and wandered over there.

"Pay attention, President Twitchell," commanded Spicer, forgetting that Coyote was no longer head of the college, "This gene transfer should allow you to acquire learned experiences from other animals. You could eat the bacteria and the new genes would transfer to your cells. If we could target stem cells— if we could get the genes into shape-shifting proteins, then they could transfer into other proteins—"

"Shape-shifting proteins? Is that what controls shape-shifting?" Coyote asked.

"No, different kind of thing. It's the same protein, it just changes shape depending on the local electromagnetic field. These proteins force the DNA to activate and the blueprint is used to develop—"

"Okay, I'm ready for the shots," Coyote said.

"No shots, the cells were in the donut you just ate. You should be changing over the next few hours. We need to discuss a few of the factors and limits, before you—"

But, Coyote had raced off.

As soon as the sun set, the blue genes started expressing themselves. Coyote had to admire himself in the mirror. This was so much more subtle and sophisticated than just being wolf-taller or having hawk-vision. This was Ur-Coyote myth legend stuff. He was massive, from the direwolf genes; his legs were so thick that they could not break when he ran. His canine teeth were so curved that they hung over his lips. His pelt was as rich as an otter, but as colorful as a tropical fish. His larger eyes could see in the dark. The penis would inspire awe when he whipped it out. Maybe he should try it, now. Then he remembered the backup systems for photosynthesis and recycling. Truly he was a work of art. Time to put it all in motion. The two big front claws tapped when he walked.

Near the city limit, he targeted the blue fluorescent image and he launched himself towards the mouse; he was running and knew he had nothing to fear this time from those awful secondary characteristics. He tracked it and scooped it up and swallowed it. He analyzed the calorimeter reading on his wrist. It indicated he had spent 43,000 kilocalories to consumer 119 kc. Hmm. At this rate he would have to eat over 361.345 mice to survive the night. He decided to get started. Too bad he wasn't better at math; he might have realized that 43,000 was the expense of catching each mouse.

"Dad," said little Mouse, "There is a neon billboard stumbling and jumping towards us!"

"Run, it's Coyzote!" and the mice hid under some leaves.

Coyote could not see them in the shadows from his glow, and he missed them both, although he gave them tremendous headaches from his pounding feet.

He knew he had to get larger prey. He searched for deer. None. He had to go towards the buffalo. He started running towards the prairie, but ran out of energy after two miles and collapsed. It was night, so the green cells were not working. The shrunken shape lay unmoving, gently flashing towards the red end of the spectrum. Pretty soon, some female fireflies were hanging around Coyote.

It was time to make another journey to the west, judged the King.
The clouds however were all moving east, and cloud-flying was his
way of getting around. That meant a long circular trip. But, first he
needed to get his staff. Yes, the world's first weapon of mass
destruction, a staff so heavy, so mighty, so long, so pregnant that it
could expand to fill the universe or dwindle to the size
of a small needle. How many heads had been broken by that iron?
Pregnant? What a funny word. He himself had been born from
a pregnant rock that had dropped a stone egg—did rock still get
pregnant, he wondered, or was he the only offspring?

   Who would be dumb enough to marry a rock?

He sighed. He had spent so much time protecting his kingdom
of monkeys from being killed by a tribe of upstart, hairless monkeys,
man. And the battle was not won, yet. He wanted to visit another
continent and see how monkeys were treated there.

Following rumors of the new gods coming out of North America,
He traveled by ship to Vancouver, then took the train to Chicago,
and then down to Kansas City.
     'What an unprepossessing temple,'
Monkey thought, 'how could they be powerful without a magnifi-
fucking-cent temple?' He knocked on the door and announced
himself, "Tis I, Monkey, Controller of the Uni-frigging-verse and
Master of Space."
    The door was opened by Sports, who was doubling
as the bouncer, "Go away, all the pedestals are full."
   Monkey tried to push his way in, but Sports pushed back,
and while he was thinking of a good insult, Monkey slipped by him.
He went directly to the largest god, Humanity, and said, "Monkey
here. I am here to join with you other inno-damn-vative gods."
    Humanity answered, sneering, "What can you do?
Simian tricks? We can see those in a zoo."
     Monkey turned around
and bared his rump at her, then raced to the food buffet. He was
stuffing food in his cheeks when Sports came in and said, "You're out
of here!" And charged. Monkey threw bananas in front of his path
and Sports was down, howling, "My quadriceps, Oh! Help, get the
Trainer! Oh, that hurts."

Monkey threw food at Humanity, threatening her august and immense body, but she gobbled it down.

"Rudeness makes a god?" asked Celebrity.

"Hey, where is my watch?" exclaimed Clock.

"Theft makes a god?" asked Celebrity.

"Why not, Hermes is a thief. Loki is a thief. With you an empty mask makes a god," Monkey answered.

"Nowadays, we expect more," said Bottomline.

"But, that's all *you* do!" said Monkey. "Look at Corpo-shit-ration there, stealing worker's retirements. Look at Humani-fucking-ty, stealing from every other species—"

There was a collective gasp from all the gods at this uppence.

"—stealing land, water, every oppor-blowing-tunity—"

Falsedream attacked then, helped by Gigadoodle. They came slapping, but Monkey threw them over and they both landed flat on the buffet, scattering food everywhere. Oil and Entertainment were circling him, but now he was throwing dung at them and they did not want to get dirtier. Sustainability appealed to Humanity, "We can't keep this up. He fights dirty. Help us."

Humanity immediately offered a concession. "Monkey, you are a wild god. We have a use for you. We need a Keeper of all Wilderness. Will you be that person?"

Advertising snickered to Megawealth and said, "Keeper of wilderness? There is none left!" And, they all laughed quietly.

Coyote was really tired and lay listlesly in bed, remembering the brief glory of his hunt. Thank heavens the green cells recharged him enough to crawl home. He asked Wakanda to bring him food, perhaps mouse soup. She did, but she insisted on telling him another story about another visiting trickster. Coyote wondered, 'what was up with that?'

Wakanda started talking about the legend of the Monkey King: "The Jade Emperor invited Monkey to Heaven and gave him a job as Keeper of the Heavenly Stables. The peace lasted a whole day, until he discovered that his post was so lowly that even the horse manure ranked higher than he. Terribly insulted, Monkey ran amok, threatening the peace of heaven. The Emperor consulted his advisors and bestowed a new title upon him: Master of Infinite Space (referring to the vacuum in Monkey's head).

'That's much better,' said Monkey, impressed. Although he was not toilet-trained or heaven-trained, Monkey thought this new title was a license to do anything. He stuffed his face with the Peaches of Immortality, defecated at official parties, and made obscene gestures to everyone. Finally, he claimed that nothing was good enough and left Heaven in disgust.

Now, the Emperor was deeply insulted and sent an army to obliterate Monkey, but Monkey defeated them with his stone essence and his martial fighting techniques. The Emperor had to call on Buddha, who had defeated Monkey once.

Buddha knew better than to use force against Monkey. He offered him a wager, instead: 'If you're so clever, jump off the palm of my hand. If you can, I'll accept the Emperor in as a monk-sans-key and give Heaven to you. But, if you can't, I'll need a full apology and painful penance.'

The Monkey King laughed and agreed.

Buddha stretched out his hand and Monkey got on, then jumped a thousand miles. He landed in a desolate plain with great columns reaching up the sky. 'Ah, the Five Pillars of Wisdom at the end of the Universe,' he thought. 'Buddha was stupid to make such a silly bet.' To show his disrespect, he pissed all over the nearest pillar and jumped back to claim his reward.

'Tell the Emp to pack his bags!' shouted Monkey as he landed, "Monk is back!"

The Holy One raised a sublime eyebrow. 'Don't grin. Look down,' he said, 'you've been on my palm the whole time.' An astonished Monkey rubbed his eyes and stared at the five pink pillars of Buddha's hand. Then he smelled the stench of monkey urine and trembled. The next thing he knew, he was lying on the ground with a mountain on top of him. He stayed there for five hundred years, being force-fed molten copper and iron.

Wakanda finished, "What did you learn from this?"

Coyote said, "Is that why no one ever shakes hands with Buddha? Look, I love these myths and stuff. What's that got to do with me?"

"Nothing, right now, but the world has other tricksters and they all seem to be roving around looking for trouble. By the way Monkey was freed to go on a pilgrimage."

Meanwhile, back in Kansas, after traveling to look over his realm of wilderness, Monkey realized it was far less than the area of athletic fields that Sports controlled.

He got in a fight with Media and broke his nose. Gofor had a bandage ready. Advertising felt for her already-battered good friend and went to Humanity with a suggestion. Humanity called to Monkey and said that Monkey could have domain over all animals also if he could defeat Coyote and bring the pelt to the new building on Olympus Street in Kansas City. She was proud that the gods were getting a new 70-story building, green design and LEED certification.

Advertising added that Monkey could have Coyote's pedestal and his seat at the Square Table (Not round, no way, what with the need to show differences in status).

So Monkey went to coyote territory and bludgeoned a few coyotes, shouting for the Big C himself. Finally, Monkey and Coyote faced off on the hill overlooking Hazel Creek.

"Tell me your name first," Coyote asked. "King, Monkey King."

"Seriously, I need to know the name of he who is going to kill me."

Monkey smiled at the admission of defeat before the first blow. "Very well, it is King Sun Wukong."

Coyote pondered, then repeated it, "Sun Wukong, King Sun Wukong, King Sunwu Kong? King Kong, oh shit, I get it! You're that ape!"

With a cry of outrage, Monkey swung his staff. Coyote ducked quickly enough, but he could not stop snickering. Wakanda had told him that 'Sun Wukong' meant 'king of space' but that this ape was only the master of his own mental vacuum.

Then the ground shook violently as the staff hit near Coyote's foot. Sun wondered if this was the laughing master pattern he was faced with, now.

He hurled the staff so hard at Coyote that it sailed out of sight. Coyote pulled out a saturday night special and blasted away at Monkey, but it did not more than slightly chip that stone exterior. Finally, with no weapons left. Monkey threw his dung at Coyote.

Badger saw that and shouted "Shit Fight!" But, that fight was a tie, also, both beasts covered in filth.

Coyote ran off to prepare another strategy. He had the yellowjacket sisters make him up as a beautiful woman, just slightly hairier and more bowlegged than human. As they combed his hair, he became transformed. Now he was a young maiden, just before her period.

She was very beautiful indeed. They dressed "her" in Wakanda's finest clothing so that she could have no rivals.

She left to seduce Monkey and reduce him to a naked, whimpering hulk. She came upon him at the corner of Main and Fish in Powhattan. Monkey was swinging from a bent lamp post. Coyote started a long sensuous strip, but before he even got the shoulder strap off, Monkey was naked and coming towards him in an clearly excited state. Coyote panicked and ran. Monkey was supposed to be humiliated by being naked in public—instead, he acted like a porn star on the set of "Kathy does Kansas.' Monkey started following him, but Coyote knew how to ditch primates, and made it home to the den, unscathed, although the hem was torn.

Wakanda saw the tear, but let Coyote ask for advice. Then, she said, "Just think of him as someone like yourself. What would trick you? Remember the story of Monkey and the monk." Coyote crossed his eyes in concentration.

The next day, in Powhattan, Coyote approached Monkey humbly, and suggested, "Look, this is going nowhere. We are too equally matched, although your staff seems mightier. How about this. You be my sidekick for a few years, then I'll be yours, and you can show me China. What do you say?"

Monkey cursed himself for not saying that first. Now, he could not angle to do it the other way, without looking weak. But could he trust this needle-nosed upstart? He asked: "Will I have a title? And pay?"

"Of course, both. Your title would be, umm, err, 'Divine Minister of Simian Ass-wiping.' Yea, that's good."

"And this ass-wiping, what does that mean?"
"Well, it's like beating people up, like a General actually."

"And the pay?"

"A thousand magic balls. They are from Africa and they turn into gold. I heard them called Mongongo nuts. What do you say?"

"They don't look like gold," Monkey said, criticizing the picture Coyote had handed him.

"Well, no, you have to eat them first, then they turn into gold when they come back out."

'This was stranger and stranger,' Monkey thought. 'Maybe, I should just agree, then I can betray him later.' Monkey demanded:

"Show me, first, immed-fucking-iately."

"Oh, from Missouri I see. Okay. I happen to have a small piece of nut with me," and Coyote flashed something brown and put it in his mouth and pretended to swallow it, "Damn, that was fine. We just have to wait a few moments and it comes out the other end."

Coyote reached under his tail and pulled out a golden band. "Simple chemistry, really, the protons get—well, it's too technical." He held out the band to Monkey, then said, "Let's see how it looks on you," and placed it on the monkey's head. "Bingo, it fits!"

And Monkey thought, 'Bongo, I'm tricked.' It was the gold head band of Tripitaka, the Buddhist monk he had to serve on many adventures and quests, battling demons and righting wrongs—and now he was in thrall to a cunning canine who ate his own poop—

"Ptooey," Coyote spit out the dung he had put in his mouth, then he spoke some words he had memorized. "Harlo bunky perpetoi. A little trick I learned from high school history class."

"Dogshit, you saw it in a movie!" and Monkey reached for the band to remove it, but it tightened. "Oh, no, not the Headache Sutra!" This was the second time in 3000 years he had to bear this torture.

Coyote saw the Monkey's eye bulge a little and started to recite the words again.

"No, wait, no need, I give up!" Monkey was fuming. He knew he could not remove it. He knew there was no defense except submission. "I will be your humble dis-frigging-ciple. I will help you!" Monkey put his hands over his eyes. The pain lessened. Monkey put the trick part of his brain to work on figuring our how to get the band off.

Coyote was smiling and nodding. The band had worked, as Wakanda had said it would. He spoke in a reconciling tone, "This is an important holy purpose to free Coyotes, Badgers, and even monkeys from the grip of human slavery. Your help is critical. Your rewards will be many. Are you ready to begin, with me, for the animals of the world?"

Monkey nodded. He remembered the last time peace had been made with Heaven and he had been granted the title of 'Buddha Victorious Against Disaster.' He was immortal, now. He could outwait, then outwit, a simple canine brain.

Coyote was biting his left front footpad vigorously, then he licked his ass (moisturizing was so important to healthy skin) and said, "Let's go! To the lab!"

121

Coyote was proud of his contest, but he resisted putting Monkey on a leash. To show he was an honorable victor, Coyote decided to liberate laboratory animals first, monkeys first.

The dungnamic duo headed towards Southern Kansas College in Wheatville. Soon, with the help of a map and an unsuspecting Freshman named Shepherd, ironically, they were able to locate the Psychology Building. Behind the pine at the edge of the building Coyote whispered to Monkey, who nodded quietly. Coyote waited as Monkey went off. He chewed on his footpad and took a nap. Monkey simply walked into the building and through the department until someone took him to the cages and put him in an empty one with a note that read, "Another one of your apes escaped. Lock the doors!"

At 4 the researchers left; at 5 the secretary left; at 5:15 the student workers left; at 5:16 Monkey opened the cage and the front door. At 5:18 Coyote strolled in eating an apple from the front desk.

"You take the hominids and rats. I'll take the dogs and cats," and Coyote headed for the cat cages, opening one after another. When they sat and looked at him, he said, "You're free, you can go now?" They ignored him.

As a father, Coyote knew just to ignore them, and as soon as he did, a few left the building, a few went to see what monkey was doing and a few stayed in the cages, finishing their grooming. He went to the dogs next and opened their doors. The first dog said, "Hey, we get fed in an hour."

"Yea," said the second one, with electrodes in his head, "come back then."

A third dog just looked at Coyote and panted happily, Coyote thought at him, but then he noticed the dog's eyes were on the clock. Coyote rolled his eyes—polluted gene pool—and went to see what Monkey was doing.

The rats were all out of their cages and looking for holes. Monkey was talking to a Bonobo animatedly. The other monkeys were still in their cages.

Coyote started to let them out, when Monkey said, "Wait, we have to know their hierarchy or they'll get into a fight."

Coyote sat patiently and listened to the two primates talk.

"I don't know how we'll adjust. We're all from forests, and I just don't see a lot of trees in this picture. Here, at least we are cared for and can see each other everyday," explained the alpha Bonobo.

Monkey nodded and reassured the other: "Well, think of it as a field trip. You can always come back, and I'm sure you will be welcomed. But, surely you as smart as hair-impaired humans. Just stand up, literally, and look around. We're going to find a place where we all can live, in com-shit-fort, unstressed, and for much longer."

Coyote grimaced for a moment, being reminded of his lies to Monkey.

Monkey continued, "So, what say you, open your cousin's cages and let's go for a walk with my friend."

The Bonobo bowed slightly to Monkey, guessing that the gold band marked him as king and Coyote was a pet of some kind, then he opened another cage and waved that monkey to open the others. Two of the chimps grabbed white coats and marched into the dog area and shut the cages with most of the dogs still inside.

Coyote could only shake his head at the sad domesticated canids, bred to be friendly, fat and dumb.

The Dung-thrower gang, lead by an ape and a coyote, followed by Bobobos, and then by a few chimpanzees, who wore white coats, walked down the center of the street, not disturbed by any cars, although a few people looking out their windows thought maybe the scientists had escaped from the College and were herding animals to the zoo. In fact, the zoo was where they were going.

"Same plan?" Coyote suggested.

"No, let's just wait until dark and go over the wall."
Coyote nodded, "We'll need keys again."

The invasion went like clockwork. Monkey and the Bonobos went to liberate the chimpanzees. Coyote went to get the coyotes, who were glad to be free. "Don't you want to wait for dinner first?" Coyote asked sarcastically.

"What? Why?" answered an old dark Coyote.
"Never mind, let's go."

"What about the wolves?" asked the dark one. Coyote gave him the keys, not wanting to get near wolves for a while. While the wolves were running at high speed for the open gate, Coyote went to see the Otter pen. Musty's friend was still there, so Coyote got her out. She indicated the cages for the Mink and weasels, and Coyote said, "Okay. Catch up to me."

Coyote regarded the other inhabitants of the zoo, who were aware of the radical changes. The elephant shook his head no, and Coyote understood that the large cats and the arctic animals would not do well on their own either. So, he went to the deer cage, then the wildcat cage, making sure that the deer—funny looking deer at that— got away first, bounding in tremendous leaps. Coyote wondered if he could even catch them at 45 miles per hour.

The coyotes and wolves had scattered as many other good wild animals did. The primates clustered around Monkey. The otter, mink and weasels followed Coyote, who decided to lead them back to Powhattan and let Otter help them. Coyote shouted to Monkey that they should split up. The Humane Societies and pet shops would have to wait until tomorrow.

The gods at their temple in Wichita, now disguised as a Masonic Lodge, so no one would ever interrupt them, got a report of animal liberation movements and figured out that it was suspect. They were concerned by any effort to upset the balance of human domination. They met in an emergency meeting to take action.

Monkey King prepares for battle

Now Coyote was ready to run for office again, on a platform of freedom and change. There were the usual problems getting in the democratic party and on the ballot, but he was ready this year, to switch to being a business green candidate.

In Stinkbeetle Plaza in central Prairiedog Town, Eagle began the debate with his opening statement, "Is Coyote good. I think we can confidently say, 'no!' He is not good. Is he good to his mate? No. Is he good at hunting? No. Is he good for anything? No. I invite my unesteemed loser to respond."

     "Allow me to respond," Coyote responded evenly, "First, I concede all of my friend Eagle's points. And he is my friend. We are both scavengers, unlike Golden Eagle and Wolf. But, does that mean Coyote has no good? Is not Coyote good *for* teaching lessons to the young.? Is not Coyote good *for* entertainment? Is not Coyote good *to* make fun of? Is not Coyote good *at* inviting chaos to visit any order? Furthermore, what is the good *of* Coyote? Balancing the desert, so there are not too many mice? Setting an example? Prepositions make all the difference in any sentence. Is Coyote good *with* words and emotions? You decide."

     "Is Coyote good with words? Does he use them to tell the truth? Or to twist the meaning back to him?" Eagle asked.

     "I think my friend Baldy is trying to be 'pedantic' or sophistic or sophomoric or moronic, or something. Truth? Please. What is truth after all: Beauty, Good, 'Words we want to hear'? No, let's go back to good, not get derailed into philosophical mush about truth. The problem with good, which was after all the question before us, is that it is just another way to grade things, to make caste systems of animals (and even humans). When we say something is good, we are quantifying them. Good is an 87 or better. But that is an abstraction, a way of reducing complex people into numbers to fit in tables to be presented as data for consumption by corporate sales—No! I say. Let us not even ask if Coyote, or Badger, or Bat, or anyone is good. Let us accept them as they are, members, contributing, working members of the community."

     Eagle paused reflectively, "My good friend Patchy Coyote wants you not to measure him by your standards, as good or bad, because he is only a 68 in the ratings game. If he were good, he would not try to confuse you. He is not good. Ask yourselves: Has Coyote hurt me recently? Has he messed up the quiet harmony of the neighborhood? You answer, please."

"I concede to my feather-headed friend—sorry, I meant featherless-headed friend—or is it headless-feathered friend?— that I may be a 68. But, what is wrong with that? Is that not the average, the gentleman's 'C' or the Bushman's best? Should I want to be better than my peers, Badger, Otter, Skunk? Would not me wanting to be better than these exemplary saltlicks of the earth make me not good? That is how I know I am good. I want to be with you, not above you. I want to be in your company, not commanding it—"

"I think he means he wants you in him, half-eaten—" Eagle began.

"Quiet please. Allow the speaker to finish," urged Stinkbeetle, the moderator.

"In the basic sense of the word, Coyote, me of course, is good. He—I—participates in the development of our fine community. Maybe you think I am bad, but then maybe you are kinder to your spouse because of that. Maybe you think I disrupt things, but maybe the community is strengthened by a little disruption, by contrast and alternatives. And who can say, over time, whether my actions make things better or worse, or if what I do is good or bad."

"But, we can make that judgment," noted Eagle, "You are bad. The community would improve without you. If you doubt that, then leave, and come back in a hundred years, heh, heh, and we can taste the difference, smell the cleaner air. What do you say?"

"It would not be scientific, and I was a scientist once, you know, because we do not have a control community, or a control coyote, to experiment with—"

"Nothing could control Coyote," Rattler hissed. Stinkbeetle released a stern toxic hiss of his own, and thumped his gavel in warning, almost squashing himself.

Coyote looked martyred, but continued, "Of course, I would always do what the community wishes, for the best of the community. But, if I go, who will reduce the strong to tears and shivers? Who will keep the game honest? Who will be free when you others are prisoners of numbers or words? Goldbeak here wants you tame, and under his claw. Is that what you want?"

"Okay," said Stinkbeetle, "Time for the lightning round. Eagle, what should we do?"

"We should share," spoke Eagle.

"Nuts," proclaimed Coyote, "Every man for himself; the stronger get more."

"Greedy people need a firm hand to be taught better," spoke Eagle.

"Greed needs the invisible hand of the market to harmonize it."

"Survival should come first," said Eagle.

"Wealth comes first—all else is trickle down."

"Technology can help us survive," said Eagle.

"Technology can do anything we can imagine."

"Limits are necessary and sacred," urged Eagle.

"Things are unlimited, the earth is inexhaustible."

"Some things are useless; we need to say enough!" cried Eagle.

"We have to maximize productivity for everything."

"Fishing is best; the rituals are important," soothed Eagle.

"Industry is best; everyone should convert to it."

"Happiness comes from being, from doing things well," sighed Eagle.

"Happiness comes from having the most and latest things."

"Nature wants us to be frugal and harmonious," concluded Eagle.

"Nature wants to be screwed big time."

"Time's up!" Stinkbeetle cried. "The round goes to Coyote. Coyote goes to the finals in the election representing the biz green party. Please thank our generous sponsors, CrackerCan and EyyonMobiGas. Good night from Stinkbeetle Plaza!"

Eagle raises a flap

The candidates from two major parties and two minor parties had agreed to be introduced together. Turtle represented the Democratic Party, Bison the Republican Party, Wolf the Independent Party, and Coyote Business Green. The four milled on stage awkwardly, until a reporter said Turtle was a hero and asked him to speak first.

"What, no, I'm just a simple Turtle," Turtle said simply, "Happy to be in his shell, comfortable with his hole, pleased to be eating grass." And, Turtle hung his head, "Don't make me into a hero. I'm just an ordinary animal, contributing to the balance of nature."

"Don't make my shell-shocked friend uncomfortable," Coyote admonished the reporter. "This balance requires shy, retiring, slow, indecisive people like Turtle, here, and his 2 children."

"Children are our most delicious natural resource," said Wolf, running his tongue across his healthy teeth.

"Precisely, Precious," said Coyote softly. Wolf was not going to ever get elected. "Bison, you are recent immigrant, from Eurasia, isn't it?" asked Coyote.

"13,000 years is recent?" Bison wondered. "You're the dwarf form of the steppe bison aren't you?"

Bison towered over Coyote and answered, "I prefer to think of myself as a keystone animal. We ate the plains to greatness when you were eating dung. We provided for all the other animals. Our eating stimulated grasses; our dung supported millions. Our trace paths made the way for trains and highways."

"What are your plans for Kansas?" Coyote asked.

"To make it part of a glorious Commons for Bison and all animals. To bring back the tall prairie and the short prairie for all."

"So, everyone else has to move to Chicago?"

"No, not prairie dogs or hawks; certainly not wolves. I see where you're going here. But, most everyone prefers big cities and crowds anyway."

Coyote felt that had gone well.

Coyote bought new clothes to look more successful, or rather the party bought the clothes. He liked being a consumer and stated that he could represent people better now that he had shopped more and seen how expensive designer names were.

He was trying on a vest as his campaign folks discussed strategies. Meeker said, "It has to be an ignorance-based campaign. The knowledge-based approach, the science-based approach has not worked. We are not scientists, we are not wise. Let's just bumble cautiously together."

"I agree," nodded Coyote, "We know little about the past, nothing about the present and less about the future; and what we do know confuses us. Admitting this frees us, but it also limits our options to radical conservation and radical change to prevent catastrophes. Maybe a scat-based plan would have more dignity."

In his first public appearance in Powhattan, Coyote had loud music and slides running in the background. It drowned out much of what he said. Sadly, people only heard some of the words: "I promise to **kill** high prices. **Americans** should not have to **give their savings to** large corporations. **Foreign investors** have for too long benefited without **risk**. **Everything** we work for must be protected. The food we **eat**. Our homes. Too much **garbage** gets thrown away. **We must** conserve. This is what we must **try to** do to avoid **collapse**."
The slides of wheat fields waving in the breeze and apple pies on the windowsills soon got out of order from the talk. Just at the word **kill** was a pic of the Kansas national guard leaving for the Middle East. Some of the voters seemed visibly upset. Possibly, Coyote had lost that district.

Coyote tried to get voter lists to prepopulate the voter content with migrating birds and insects.

The first television interview on Channel WHAT went well:
"And, you, Candidate Coyote. Boxers or briefs?" asked Annetta Funk.

"Neither," said Coyote briefly.

"Well, what—? You know, we have not caught you having sex with any of your campaigners or prostitutes; is that because you masturbate frequently?"

"Yes, whenever I can. It relieves tension."

"But, don't you know—that is, I mean—"
"Next question."

"Left or right hand?" Funk asked, smiling.
"Neither," Coyote smiled back.

The press was frustrated. How could— uh, uh, they decided as one, not to go in that direction. Coyote had his mouth open ready to answer.

He paused and looked intimately into the lense: "I want to address the viewer directly, now," Coyote said. "I want to speak to you intimately, more so than any author friend or family, about your possessions and actions, your sexuality. Look at me, what a catch I am. More than just a face to vote for. Don't any of you women want to write to me, go on a date, take off your clothes and mate? C'mon. I can make like a wolf, or a rattlesnake. Unlike your Viagra-pumped mate, I have a bone that holds up much longer. What do you think? Ever gone a round with an immortal dog?" Coyote went wink, wink, but the viewers could not see that, since the tape went to commercial at 'mate.'

Meanwhile, Ben Helmetstraw of UNN was asking: "Have you ever killed anyone?"

"For justice or for a meal? Who died so that you could get that meat stain on your tie?" Coyote asked.

Helmetstraw looked at his tie curved over his belly and thought: 'Now how did he know what that stain was?'

Coyote smelled it of course; the cow smell lead him to the tie. "What are you thinking about Taxes?" Helmetstraw recovered.

"I cannot decide whether to tax the ugly or the beautiful. I think the beautiful; although there are fewer of them, they are often richer. Look here in this college mag, *Sewanee News*, how all the old men have young wives. Those are taxable assets!"

Marsha Stanwick of SNN tossed out a question, "Now that Bison is surging in the polls, what will you do?

"My opponent claims to be a maverick, that is, basically a stray calf, in danger of falling over the edge of a precipice and breaking its leg or being picked off by a coyote. We know he is more like an aging cow, but there isn't a name for a stray cow, unless it's hamburger. Isn't there something we can do to get him safely back to the herd? Maybe by pointing out that his ideas are strictly herd ideas? Maybe I'm wrong, maybe his ideas are different, that is, unethical, greedy and short-sighted, and he needs to take up the ideas and values of normal working people, those of us without the many or free houses, without the freedom to wallow in the public trough for money, clothing, privileges, and services. Maverick? No. Cud-chewer in a herd? Yes."

"Does Turtle have a chance?" asked Stanwick.

"My opponent points to his war record. We must not mistake survival for courage; we must not think imagination is a substitute for experience. We must not pretend that experience is a substitute for intelligence. And we must not respect intelligence without action. This is why I am the better candidate. I have avoided imagination, experience, and intelligence, just to be qualified for this moment!"

The press had a good time with Coyote, taking quotes out of context. Sheila Rentdrop of Fox News (the other one) asked Coyote about Bison's plan.

Coyote responded, "I don't give a 10-dollar bill, I don't even give a buffalo nickel about that plan."

Martha Stalwart of MSSNBC asked Coyote to summarize his platform in one simple, direct paragraph.

"I want you," Coyote winked, "to join the business green party, the party party. We can legalize pot and all drugs. We can legalize prostitution; make it safe for everyone, with licensed medical care and benefits for the ho's. We can legalize gambling, and then get rid of all the rest of the taxes, except on gambling. No tax on profits for corporations, just salaries and stock payments, except when they gamble. We can also get rid of schools higher than the 8th grade. No reason to go higher, just have a lot of apprenticeships, so professors can make as much as plumbers."

Kathy Sweetbriar of the Wireless News opined, "Coyote just wants the dog vote, as he is one."

"I'm not a dog," Coyote declared, "dogs are the sickest of species, and recessive genes lead to a recessive species. That is one reason why I mate with as many females as possible—to bring wholes genes back into that sad species."

"What are some of the problems?" Sweetbriar asked lamely.

"Lameness, heart attacks, blindness, and hundreds more problems. This is from the length of domestication. Wolves, heh heh, were the first animals ever domesticated. Wolves, not Coyotes. And, inbreeding to try to make wieners or giants has caused these problems."

Jim Geoni of The Raw Onion asked Coyote about the stock market.

"Green is the new black, white is the new red," Coyote propounded.

Madonna Lumplumpinini asked Coyote to deliver a ringing metaphor for his campaign.

Coyote obliged: "We must fight the good

race, sell the ball to the goal and light fires to fill the sails of progress. We must stay the course and dream the unbearable dream to nurture the strength of many to reward the sustainability of the few."

In Citibank Arena, Coyote gave his final speech the night before the vote, challenging the people with true honesty and false modesty:

"What is the political truth of this campaign? That we are great selfless leaders? Or, that both of us are power-hungry grubs looking for a body to infest, to further fulfill our own self-interest? Why nothing could be further from the truth. That is why I am willing to give everything I have to charity, and I urge my opponent to do the same. Only when I am as poor as the poorest of the people, will I be qualified to capture your trust and to lead you into a shining future. I will be the glue that holds together our towering inferno. I will be the rope that hangs us to the tree, I will be the balloon that raises our hot air. Trust me and the trillions of dollars will be our debt forever. I am here only out of crass self-interest. I will not do anything that will not benefit me first. Why? Because, I need to try things first. That is the genius of a leader—to test massive wealth first to make sure it is safe and desirable for everyone!"

Coyote paused for effect.

"Let's sing: To speak the unspeakable truth, to dare the undareable path. That is my quest, to be richer than you, to … ahh, you know what I mean—never mind."

Coyote paused again and became seriouser.

"Everyone needs to be special, to be completely unique. Why, when I gaze over you, milling in the lowing herd, chewing your cuds, I see how really different you are, how some of you have been branded yourselves with tattoos that use different color inks and have different kinds of wings or words, how others have cut and dyed your hair differently with purple and pink, and how many of you wear your jeans with your sport coats or tee-shirts and some of you keep wearing them even with gaping rips and tears made by machines. You are not losers! You are not normal! You are special! You should not need to work, to do anything productive. You should not have to contribute to the bland horizon of society. You are valuable as you and your life should be dedicated to cultivating that difference so others can appreciate the unique perspective of the universe that is you. And, as your senator, I will work tastelessly and effortlessly to promote you on your behalf.

My opponent says you are lemmings, drawn to the sea

by the taste of salt, but I say you are tasteless and don't even know the sea is there! My opponent says you are ants in a hill droning on with your chores, but I say you are all queens and should be waited on by machines with heated cushions. My opponent says you have *failed miserably* to be responsible, hard-working, ethical individuals, but I say you have failed *spectacularly*! Don't be desperate to succeed, you have already succeeded beyond any ant or cow. Don't be afraid to do what you want, others are working to support you. So, let's come up with good ideas for ruling the earth. Let's work on Web4 or Gameboy9! Let's design a better recliner and a faster car to put it in! I am for a positive future, one not shackled by the dead hand of the past, not limited by the blindered eye of the present. Let's go! Now!! Vote Coyote!!!"

The herd mooed and surged towards Coyote, and he basked in their worship.

Coyote was careful to appear to be working dramatically hard in the final days, wiping his brow and tossing pieces of paper to underlings or coworkers, sitting with his tie loose and threadbare feet on the desk. Then, he won by 844 votes.

He gave his victory speech; he was so excited, he could barely remember what he said: "Winning is never enough! You have to look forward to … more winning, to the other rewards, not just money, but houses and jewels … But, these guys here on the podium with me, these fine political warriors [sniff] need someone to lead [sniff] them — that would be me. And, you, little people, thank you for your love and support. Good night! [sniff]"

He took off the Johnny Depp mask and relaxed. He looked over at the Al Gore plaster mask and wished that it had come in latex—perhaps it would have been too expressive. Finally, he was going to Washington, well, after the mandatory recount anyway. The bull was his! He had the horns in his hands. He would make laws and funnel wealth where it was meant to go. Now, if he could just survive the next two months!

The CVA planted rumors about Fox and Coyote being terrorists, as well as Coyote's involvement in the disastrous Operation Coyote in Tucson and the Flaming Shitbag Mission in Spokane. This guaranteed the involvement of the Houseland Security Department (HoSeD) and the Kansas Natural Guard (K-NaG).

The CVA was concerned that Coyote would have too much power as a Congressman. They had planted information about voting irregularities and illegal contributions to Coyote's campaign. Gigadoodle was working on the mandatory recount for the election, manufacturing new votes for the Republican party.

The CVA also sent a representative, Eagle, the most respected of animals, to the secret Masonic Headquarters of the new gods—doubly secret because the new gods dominated the old white geezers—in Wichita with information about Coyote's whereabouts near Powhattan.

HoSeD was first on the scene, prepared to fight, then investigate. "General Tankbuster, sir, thanks to your wise leadership, we are ready to FLUB."

"Ah, yes," Tankbuster replied, although he was always put off by the acronym for his plans for urban warfare, Fighting Lengthy Urban Battles. Powhattan would be a good test, a small test anyway. "Are we using MISCUE in this operation?"

Major Frink answered gravely, "No, sir, Admiral Belcher felt that there was not enough lead time for Military Intelligence for Starting Counter Underground Efforts at this time, sir."

Tankbuster nodded, but resented some waterdog making landside decisions. "What about the Greywater contractors?"

"You mean mercenaries?" Frink asked.

"Guards, whatever."

"We're not sure where they are, now. When we approached them with a contract, they panicked and opened fire on Congressman Blecher and his staff."

"Shit, doesn't any—what about the military scientists from Koors College? Are they working on C1ND1?"

"Yes, sir, on the computer, M1L1E, sir!"

"What the hell does that stand for?"

"Military 1 Lightspeed 1 Eco-computer, I think."

Coyote had been alerted about possible actions, so he met with Monkey again. In a move not even he understood, he removed the gold braid from Monkey's head and gave it to him, "You might want to go back to China, before things get too hot here. I heard the industrial Gods and the Military are gearing up for a war to end all wars."

Monkey played with the braid, not expecting to be out of captivity so soon. Even the old Buddhist monk had not been so kind. "Perhaps I could 'liberate' some of the soldiers to even things out. Besides, I have some unresolved issues with these new gods, who have judged me not good enough for their ranks."

"Well, don't do anything that is not fun. We are both warriors for the unrepresented. Hey, why don't you come over for dinner tonight?"

"Thank you, perhaps in a week or so. I have to practice a few tricks of my own," and he waved goodbye.

Coyote went back to staring at the computer screen, planning his own tricks.

"What have you got for us, Snakthorn?"

"Well, sirs, as you know we have been training dolphins to deliver explosives and attach them to ships."

"This is the desert, need I remind you."

"Yes, sir. Grasslands, sir. We may have to provide wet suits for them, or if we flooded the prairie then we could release them."

"Seriously?"

"Well, it's a thought."

"What do you have, Commander Whetnurs?"

"UP-URS, sir!"

"What?"

"The projects, sir, Urban Pacification Using Reducing Sound, that we tested in the desert on animals, like coyotes."

"What about it? Didn't it turn them to dust?"

"No, sir. DUST is Destruction of Uncooperative Surface Targets. That was the WAMBAM ADDONS and UP-URS, sir." Whetnurs remembered the Weapons for Arbitrary Mass-destruction and the Biological Amplification Monitor for the Acoustic Detection,

Destruction Or Neutralization System and the Biological Amplification Monitor for the Acoustic Detection, Destruction Or Neutralization System.

"What about Coyote?"

"He was the target."

"No, what about the strategy?"

"Oh, that was Counter Operational Yoke for Obstructionist and Terrorist Entrapment. It was part of SNUF, you know, Systems for Neutralizing Undefined Foes."

"Did we decommission the Anti-Suicide Stations for Holding Operatives and Lethal Explosives (ASSHOLEs) and the ViSIT-Hors (Virtual Sensory Isolating Temporal Helmets) from the last debacle?"

"Yes, sir!"

"Are there any letters we have not used?"

"Yes, sir: Z, X, J, K."

"Hmmm, what about Zapping Xeric Kansas Jacks?"

"Yes, sir, that's good. I was thinking of Killing Xanthic Zipper Jammers. But, yours is better, really."

"HMMM."

"His Majesty's Merchant Marine. Sir?"

"No, Cpl, I was just thinking."

Cpl. Menshun finished his Outline the Battle: Months of prep, weeks of movement of materials and men, days of positioning and posturing, hours of orders and instructions, for minutes of bombing the shit out of a few hills in Kansas. That's the way it happened. Awesome explosions.

"I wish it were that simple, Munchkin. Animals had been tracked by satellite in infrared. Smart weapons were programmed, pointed and launched. Receivers recorded the damage."

Two hummers approached the moonscape. The men who got out were wearing exoskeletons and carrying sonic disruptors. Main street was hit worst; most of the buildings had been skeletonized. Urban renewal would be much easier now. They called for the main force.

"Okay, men, everyone vested, ha, ha."

And everyone laughed automatically, two 'ha's exactly, knowing that Sergeant Hammer meant the warfighters' wardrobe, with new armored vests, equipped with removable throat and groin protectors, front and back removable plates, and a metal Frisbee. These suits were marvelous. Each one had a global positioning system, stealth and night-vision devices, improved digital communications systems, remote controls, more precise sensor systems, reference books for identifying military vehicles and soldier profiles (Downloadable Information Manager With Intellectual Technologies), and cup-holder. The uniforms had built-in chemical-biological protection, embedded with electric wires and fiber optics that communicated with their Avatars on the military computer M1L1E. They were waterproof and flame-resistant, with built-in insect repellent, antibacterial agents for treating injuries, and even antimicrobial agents to make the soldiers bodies smell like a grassland after a light summer rain. Ahh. Even the dog-tags had chips now to report all data back to the central computer.

"I can't move, sir."

"Dammit, I told you to put on the exoskeleton first! Dickson, help sluggo here. Everyone got their Moles?"

They nodded. The MOdular Load-bearing Equipment was a modular rucksack with removable compartments and components, and fighting load vest that had removable pockets for the Rifleman, Pistol, Squad Automatic Weapon (SAW), Gunner, and Grenadier configurations.

"Striker Brigade, Radar scopes?"

"Check," The men knew they could see through a foot of concrete with those. So it should work with a few dirt burrows.

"M16-A2s?"

"Check."

"Clinton, you have the portable howitzer?"

"Check."

"Wetbacker, Wiltsoon, and Wamfaloon, are your SWORDS erect?

"Check." The three smiled and held hands with their special armed robot battle buddies, the Special Weapons Observation Reconnaissance Detection Systems. These robots were marvelous. They were fully autonomous with computer personalities and could move as gracefully as the soldiers and chew gum while walking.

"Okay, everyone carrying FFFFFFs?"

Everyone knew the Future Food for Field Feeding of Furtive Fighters combat rations; it even had yoghurt and chocolate.

"What about the SSSSSs?"

Everyone had their Self-sustaining Soldier Scrubbing Shower System.

"Evans, you have the 'Humvee in a box' charged?"

"Sir!" The HMMWV had hyper-velocity Kinetic Energy Missiles, a resupply trailer, and a second generation FLIR/TV acquisition system. The LOSAT system was a highly mobile, all-weather, day/night, up/down, direct-fire, anti-armor system capable of defeating threat forces at a range of several kilometers.

"Skink, you are in charge of the 'city in a box.'"

"Sir!" That was the Tent Erection Automated System Extender.

"Helm, you have the MAUVE"

"Sir!" The Manned Aerial Unmanned Vehicle Exporter.

Sergeant Hammer nodded. The Warfighters Urban Force would meet the enemy with lightweight lethality overmatch, extended range capability, the ability to defeat defilade targets, interface with the Warrior System comPuter (WaSp), and incorporate a multifunctional fire control system that provided day, night, and all weather capabilities—all for a scrawny coyote and some animals. He smiled and petted his own weapon, the Shoulder-Mounted Assault System Holder, an insanely brutal thermobaric mixture which ignited the air, producing a shockwave of unparalleled destructive power, especially against buildings or sloths. It was the epitome of THermobaric Urban Destruction. Keep collateral damage to a minimum with precision bombs? Fuck. He knew that the massive brutality of disproportionate force would leave lasting memories and lasting craters. It would take out soldiers, civilians and beauty pageant contestants. People were always screaming about protocol and innocence. Well, this would shut them up.

At WaSp center under Mt. Mulberry, Cpl. Menshun was arresting Major Barker, helped by 3 MPs, Joe Ryan, John Ryan, and Jim Ryan (unrelated). "I'm sorry sir;, it's a precautionary measure. We are concerned about being infiltrated."

      "God-dammit, stop pulling on my nose and cheek! I'm not hiding anything."

      "Sorry, sir, just have to be sure. We're escorting you to a holding facility, just for a day. Ryan, move him out."

  "Sir!" "Sir!" "Sir!" came immediate responses.
In the pen, Major Barker recognized some of the men, Cpl. Piszer, Sgt. Reeker, and 2 civilian programmers, Mat Hatter and Pat Howler. He introduced himself to the others, wondering what suspicious thing they all had in common.

Down the hallway, actually 23 hallways, Snakthorn was making sure that the computer was programmed and all the soldiers' avatars were on-line and real-time. The 3-D holographic output was phenomenally detailed, with input from GPS units showing the topography of the area. This was some 22nd-century shit. He checked everything, form by form. But, he didn't notice that there were two Pat Ryans and two Rayalta Kreelers—he just assumed the men had moved during the hour-long count.

"Okay, men, get in the Bradley Urban Fire Fighting Yokes and we'll be off. I'll be behind in the Crusher," said Hammer.

      The men were confident.
They had all trained in the Engagement Army Skills Yard and the Virtual Interactive Combat Training Imperative Machines.
Their confidence was rewarded. Within three hours after deployment, they had reports of Coyote from the unmanned glider, Raven.

  "We have him on radar, sir," announced Cpl Rumancoke. "Target and—"

    "Opps, he's gone."

      "Switch to infrared," ordered Hammer.
"There he is—opps, where'd he go?"

      "Switch to the cryptometer, see if there are air current disturbances."

    "No sir, nothing that doesn't look like grass or trees."

"Damn, figure his last speed and shoot where he will be in 20 seconds."

      "Yes, sir." Cpl Rumancoke set up his M-107 long-range sniper rifle and fired.

            "Doesn't look like it. Go 6 feet from where he disappeared and shoot there."

                  "No blood sir, no evidence of a hit."

"Hmm. Get me elevations and shoot into the nearest depression."

Coyote had lowered his body temperature and lay down. A bullet plowed into the rise in front of him. He rolled on his side and took a nap. He dreamed that Loki plucked out his eyes, so he turned over, his World of Warcraft Troll mask in the dirt.

Warrior and Doom, monitored remotely by Gigadoodle and Falsedream, had been following Coyote by his footprints. They saw Trapper Bob hiding behind a shrub, near a poorly disguised trap, but they just shrugged, not their concern.

"Sir, our Avatars are reporting that we are being attacked by invisible, titanium androids. Might be Cuban. What shall we do?"

      Sgt. Baker previewed his own screen and saw the Avatars on the ground rolled into balls like Armadillos, "Okay men, hit the ground and curl up, until I give the signal."

"Goddammit!" thundered Sgt. Hammer. "I'm going to kill something," as he lifted SMASH to his shoulder and pressed the first button. He hated calling them buttons, reminded him of his wife's blouse or something; they should be called 'kill-punches' or something. Then it fired and laid down a flat runway of destruction right through Beallringer squad and Slash squad and exploded next to Doom, who fell to bits.

      Gigadoodle said: "Damn, we lost a good god, there. I think we should have coordinated with the K-nag people. Get Warrior out now!"

      "He's not responding, but his tags are green," said Falsedream.

Coyote was looking at that glowing tag from behind a hill. How could he have been followed?—oh, footprints; how basic was that? Was he getting too technical? He raised himself up to surrender, then saw Warrior raise and aim his gun, only to be blasted off his feet by

Fox. Coyote quickly raised his gun and shot in the air—the bullet landed miles away on Snakthorn's index finger, removing it painfully. Snakthorn whimpered, "How? Why?" and cradled his finger. That would be good for a Purple Heart.

Fox quickly knocked Warrior out and bound his legs with tourniquets to stop the bleeding. Warrior would live and get a Purple Star and artificial cybernetic, turbo feet. Surprisingly, the military was becoming more colorful, getting away from silvers and golds and more towards pastels and earthtones.

Kick and Player, positioned as snipers, shot Coyote from behind.

"Confirmed kill," Kick reported, but the report went unreceived since their avatars were on the ground lying in a fetal position. They were lying on another hill, wearing shorts, shoeless, with just a gun and mic.

Player said, "You bring the sun lotion?"

"Yea, here. Let's wait for orders. There's wrong and there's Army Wrong!" and they clapped low fives.

Fox crept stealthily over to his friend and lay with his head on Coyote's stomach. He figured he would have to jump over him again, but might as well rest and look at how the battle was taking shape.

Raven was looking over the field when a large black bird with large stiff wings whizzed by him. It said 'Raven' on the side. Raven followed and tried to land on one wing, but it tumbled down and hit the ground. Raven landed near by and picked at a few warm pieces. Maybe he would take the shiniest one home for Madge.

The whole battle was also being observed by Gamer and Sports, one for ideas, the other to destroy Coyote eventually.

"I want three squads out on the ground," barked Commander Catarrini, "Get over by the creek!"

"What shall we do, sir."

"Drop your pants and moon them. They can't stand it; it'll drive 'em crazy. Then drop and curl up to avoid return fire." He got on the phone and said, "Withdraw all the forces back to Topeka and have them work on the bridges and streets until we can figure this out. For gods' sake get, General Toastmaster to review this whole debacle. I want deniability and I want it *now!*" Monkey brushed his remaining facial hairs—a Vandyke, how regal. 'Well, I'll be a human's uncle,' he thought, 'this is fun.' He wondered where Coyote was.

In all the swirling dust, Wakanda thought she saw the four racecar drivers of the apocalypse. Nos. 6, 8, 33 and 46. Number 6 on fire, 8 a skeleton—

—then, Rage squad captured Wakanda before she could reach her primary target. Before she had entered the skirmish, however, she had reported the violations of building codes and tax laws by the new owners of a new skyscraper in Kansas City, registered to Humanity, Oil & Co.

"Sir, we found Cpl. Kreeler, but we already have a Cpl. Kreeler. I didn't know what to do, so we put them both in the examination containment room."

"Good thinking, Spritzer."

They keep her in a special room with the woman she was imitating. Although she could turn invisible, they could track her by heat and movement. Wakanda knew she only had ten minutes before they could interrogate her, maybe waterboard her, hood her, and give her to the dogs. She considered all the options, including somehow changing the real Kreeler, but then decided to try something else. No one could figure out how, but her signs just vanished. Kreeler was no help.

Coyote's avatar, who wore the mask of Halo 3 Master Chief, was playing in the army central computer, targeting other units. He sent mail to each unit that the others had surrendered to the Canadian peacekeepers from the UN, who had been called in by Jimmy Carter and Mikhail Gorbachev. The avatar had noticed when Coyote had died, but had not been affected himself. That was interesting.

Fox finally decided he had to get this over with, so he jumped over Coyote and brought him back to life.

"Good work, Foxy!" Coyote slapped his friend on the shoulder. He then proceeded to pull down Warrior's pants. "C'mon, let's do the rest of them! Maybe we can line them up, you know, so—"

But, Fox had had enough revenge and left Coyote to administer the thrill of defeat. Fox saw Monkey, sitting on a hill, and introduced himself. The battle was over, so they made a bet on how long the soldiers would lie there curled up.

Time-shifting Bitch

Wakanda was sitting on a rock looking east, over the prairie.
She knew how easy it was now to rearrange her skin and muscles,
even her mass and charge. But, she wondered if time could be
manipulated as easily. She tried first to go back 200 heart beats.
Maybe if she had some kind of marker, before-event and after-event.
Maybe the metaphor of walking backwards would work.

She stepped back to North America just after the ice age. Cold winds
came off the ice. The wind was fast and cold; it took the heat from her,
so she had to shiver and huddle. It was so dry, it took the water out
of her.
    Mammoths walked with humped heads, high shoulders and
sloping backs, bodies covered in dense black hair. They were in
a family group, lead by an old female. In the distance, she saw a herd
of long-horned bison. Something large, maybe a direwolf or short-
faced bear, was slinking around the herd.
                                    In the sky were two large
black birds gliding, like a vulture or condor, against the grey fast
clouds.
    There were some coarse bushes and grasses, but almost no trees.
Wakanda was freezing. She looked for a sheltered place or a cave.
Finding nothing, she realized that she could not survive in this time
for more than a few moments, so she shifted back to 2009.

She started walking forwards, but that did not put her in the future,
just the extended present. She imagined the sun coming up again
and crossing the sky and again and again until the shuttered motion
became a constant blur. She achieved this by spinning wildly. Then,
she was falling.
                    She looked up and saw a large pyramidal building in
the distance, reflecting the sun, perhaps an arcology. She did not see
any power lines or roads, which made everything see so much larger.
Grasses extended in all directions. She looked into the bunchgrasses,
listening for the movements of mice. When she heard what she
wanted, she pounced and landed with her front feet. Then threw
a stunned mouse into the air, playing with it, catching it and eating it.
After a few more, she lay down and enjoyed the sun and clear air.
She wondered if she should walk towards the city, but decided to
enjoy the present and wait for another day to explore.

Wakanda looked and saw the sacredness that ran through everything. She understood the spiral of time, how it laid down history but denied it with repetition. After thinking about it for a while, she learned she could change without moving, then she could channel one time after another, like layers over each other, and see this spot 18,000 years ago and 4000 years into the future, as well as the present or any thread of time at all.

At first it was confusing. If she made the layers all alike, it was hard to focus on one. So, she made the present slightly brighter and graded time. The streams were going at different speeds. She realized that that had to do with her interest in them, the least interesting changing the least or the slowest. A large cat pounced at her image in one time, so she made herself invisible. She wondered how many streams she could add? How many she could participate in at the same time? She had to learn to funnel them, to keep a central focus but be able to step to either side or up or down.

She wound down the streams and settled into the field outside Powhattan. There was a light rain and she enjoyed the feel of it. She wondered if Coyote was working on a mask.

In fact, Coyote was sitting at home with the Otters, regaling them with stories of his heroism and close-calls. Otter plied Coyote with chips and beer, as Coyote described in detail how he saved Fox and Monkey. Otter was true friend.

Coyote's avatar had slipped into the NASA computers and was participating in a virtual Mars landing using his new mask, Colonel Pumpflud. It was so easy to make masks with bits. He noticed that the flesh Coyote was sending data again. Maybe he would send him email later and show him what he could do in virtual space.

Grace Sheauga: "I am sorry to hear about Violet Reason. I enjoyed some of her work. Who was she?"

Yulalona Lopez: "An enigma. A homeless doctor. An absentee mother. A brilliant loser. She wanted to make sure every patient had a good death; and she did, regardless of the cost to her. She wanted to be free of possessions and travel whenever and wherever she wanted, so she did. She wanted to write about homelessness, hopelessness and death, so, she did. Coyote was one of the losers she wanted to reinvent, from the Native American lore. She first heard the traditional stories from my father."

S: "What about your father? Where is he?"

Y: "Still on the rez. Things are better now. He just found some oak library tables at a sale, cut them up and put the wood down as flooring in his trailer. He likes working in wood."

S: "What about you? Did you resent him? Her?"

Y: "I was more interested in reinventing than resenting. I do not resent anything or anyone, not relatives, parents, hurricanes, earthquakes, or even machine economics and financial chaos."

S: "Why did you start writing about Coyote? I mean, as more than tradition, but as an extension or updating of the native stories?"

Y: "So much I have written about coyote has been lost, fled from me like images from a dream on waking. So much comes and goes in instants and evaporates back into the verbosphere, so to speak."

S: "So much was said in your earlier books about boundaries. What is important about boundaries?"

Y: "A boundary is a limit, and limits are important, not just as a characteristic of a system, but as membranes that allow the universe to work in small pieces. The most important boundary that Coyote can cross is that separating the old from the new culture, from the culture of firelight stories to the one with nuclear physics, quarks and nothingness."

S: "Don't you feel guilty about having Coyote stick his nose in every small corner of industrial modern culture? He is after all just an animal."

Y: "Traditionally, Coyote stuck his nose in everything. Coyote has dipped his nose into every science, nor matter how injudiciously; he has dipped his toe into every art, and for the humanities, coyote dipped another part of his anatomy, where it had no business.

S: "But, presenting his own dung as art? Isn't that too much?"

Y: "Well, no, because he is reflecting human society. Kitsch is respectable. Nostalgia is required. Everything 'so five-seconds ago' is now collectible, even every instance of waste or thrown-away anger carvings. Meanings are reinvented by marketeers and everything becomes important and artistically designed."

S: "I still think it can be stupid."

Y: "Case in point. Is that an elk turd around your neck, dipped in plastic, hanging from a gold chain?"

S: "My brother makes them. They're amulets for hunters."

Y: "Did you know that elk? Was it sacred?"

S: "No, but it can transform things."

Y: "Like a catalyst? Coyote is a catalyst in the education of youth."

S: "But, why doesn't he learn from his actions?"

Y: "Because the nature of a catalyst is to remain unchanged after the transformation of the other."

S: "But, Coyote does change, learn, develop."

Y: "Only in the sense of learning new things to be clever with, so he can try 'heroically' to stay the same in changing circumstances. If we learn from the character, then we may learn to change gracefully."

S: "Coyote has many elements of a modern hero."

Y: "Perhaps I misspoke. Heroes, and especially warriors, are degenerate distortions of hunters by cultures who have forgotten how to hunt, but need to protect their cows. Coyote is neither hero nor warrior."

S: "This cannot be right. My people had warriors."

Y: "True, but only after the destruction of your hunting culture and the growth of farming. Don't feel badly, it happened to many cultures, from the Navajo and Hopi to the Chickasaw and Wampanoag. This led to wars between people who had never had wars. Before that, they had leaders, wise elders and hunters."

S: "Warrior culture is still alive and vital, even in Euro society. Well, let's disagree about that later. Are you saying that killing is bad?"

Y: "No, killing is necessary to eat, but we don't kill righteously anymore, with respect and ceremonies, we just slaughter. Coyote is a hero only in the sense of being the lesson for what we should *not* do. Notice that Coyote does not have an extended family—no parents, no aunts and uncles. He has never gone through group recognition and celebration of the phases of his life, the ones that mark the change to maturity. He was never sponsored or mentored into real mysteries, hence he always acts like a selfish adolescent.

This is what happens when a culture ignores the life stages and passages of its people. We are already the most baby-like of species. We need to have our cultures tell stories and provide rites that explain why we cannot keep acting like babies in all things and have to become mature socially."

S: "Don't you worry that these stories are too graphic for children?"

Y: "We are shielded foolishly from sex and death in our culture. Pretending that hamburger comes from a warehouse and not a cow is foolish, and it leads to states of mind that allow far greater violence against living beings, because there is no connection, no responsibility, and no feeling for them."

S: "So, we should expose them to everything?"

Y: "Yes, in context, for instance, either of hunting or butchering, or of love-making and passion—but not out of context, not through body-count games or come-count pornography! We have to recover an understanding that the world surrounds us with invisible, powerful, conscious beings in natural forms. Our souls demand these, and we are already trying to get back to them with games and sports, art, diet, and ecology."

S: "Won't that work?"

Y: "No, it has to be in the context of a whole culture. We have been losing that over many, many generations. We need to piece that together again."

S: "And, we can do that through stories? How should we read Coyote?"

Y: "It would be better to hear about him through stories, speakers and listeners circled around a fire. We need to remember the intimate joys of conversing with others inside a wall of light. This is what I want to recapture."

Prerelease Review, by Claude-Marc Merleau-Ponty

In this book, fiction + myth = fith. And, plagiarism + fact = plac. Therefore, fith + plac = plith. The book is a pithy plith about a time of endless times and untimely ends. It seems somehow lifelike, without the organic mess, in its analysis of decadence and its impact on civilization. There is more than just intellectual playfulness, there is absurd playfulness, *divertissement*. The world cannot be made safe by play, however, and the gods cannot be appeased by it.

    The book takes the form of an allegory of debasement. The innocent and cruel misuse of mythology and folk-wisdom becomes a vicious attack on the essence of capitalism and *la condition humaine*. The all-too-human incapacity to regard the lives of those who fall outside the border of imagination or *Je ne sais quoi* is expressed in the adventures of Coyote and his friends. Lopez is a militant in the war for common sense and peace through making fun of and insulting everyone.

    This book dares to challenge the reader with complex genetic science and the medical implications of farting. It dares to force us to find humor in military engineering and the politics of the industrial economic bubble. These things are not funny! They are *les boules*. Then it ties us down and force-feeds us big words *portemanteaux* and caustic mythology. And, finally, when we are nauseous, it offers us the tonic of talking animals and stupid human tricks. And, with the last burp of relief, all that is left is the vaporous image of an immortal dog mooning us. What kind of person would read this book?

    What kind of person would write it? Think Steven Hawking and Kurt Vonnegut sharing a body. Perhaps Jorge Luis Borges sharing a brain with Linus Pauling. Or Woody Allen and Black Hawk on the same bus. Okay, Sherman Alexie and Alan Greenspan in the same paragraph? Or Diderot and Hugues Guérin, if you will.

    In fact, the depth of scholarship and breadth of humor lead me to a *soupcon* that she is not just one person, but *casque* of writers trying to *floof* us. Why are they hiding behind one mask? Are they ashamed? There seems to be no *appellation contrôlée*. Does Lopez even exist? We must *cherchez la femme*. Is she ashamed of her identities? Why am I going on without editing? What do you mean we're out of space—*C'est agité*. *J'accuse* you literary fascists! This will never be a best seller! *Bien fait*! *C'est châteaux en Espagne. Ceux qui rient le vendredi, pleureront le dimanche—*

About the Author

Yulalona Lopez has a Harvard degree in Astronomy. The result of an unlikely alliance between a Tonoho O'odham man and a Gaelic woman, she now earns her living as an investor in Grants Pass, Oregon, where she follows coyotes on their errands in and out of town. She is the autor of several earlier books, including *Tropomorphoses*, *Night Wolves*, and *Coyote Remasked* (and co-author of *Coyote Redivivus* and *Coyote Redux*).

Colophon
Within sight of a Coyote on Tallevast Road
In the Blue Oak Bus in Manatee County
On a Borrowed Ibook
Using Indesign and Adobe Caslon Pro
to print on recycled paper
with primitive images by RianGarciaCalusa

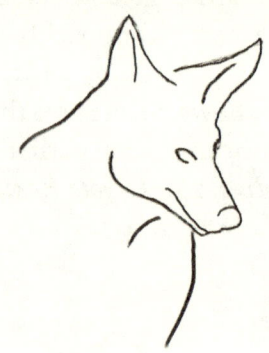

www.ingramcontent.com/pod-product-compliance
Lightning Source LLC
Chambersburg PA
CBHW030614130626
46552CB00002B/568